NEW BRIGHTON

Rachel's Story

by

M. Susan Thuillard

Bloomington, IN Milton Keynes, UK

AuthorHouse™
1663 Liberty Drive, Suite 200
Bloomington, IN 47403
www.authorhouse.com
Phone: 1-800-839-8640

AuthorHouse™ UK Ltd.
500 Avebury Boulevard
Central Milton Keynes, MK9 2BE
www.authorhouse.co.uk
Phone: 08001974150

First published by AuthorHouse 2/7/2006

ISBN: 1-4259-0880-2 (sc)

*Printed in the United States of America
Bloomington, Indiana*

This book is printed on acid-free paper.

No matter what evil or good may be our lot in life, forgiveness and love will triumph in the end.

Contents

Prologue

Somewhere in the mists of time and space, lives crossed the meridian of existence. Levels of consciousness and living crossed barriers of heaven and the universe to become one. For the briefest interval, the lives of separate centuries touched and an Illusion was born.

It is said there is a window through which one might cross to another time. If that is true, perhaps Rachel's Story validates the Illusion of a future era. The energy of her youthful faith may have been the catalyst between reality and apparition, between the spirit of Julie Kincaid and the spirit of Marianne Armstrong...

One

The Black Beginning

The young woman ran blindly into the cold, dark forest. Still wet and shivering from swimming across the muddy river, she climbed higher onto the mountains, feeling her way in the inky darkness of a moonless night. She stumbled and slid in the dirt, scraping and scratching her already tender skin. Brambles and briars seemed to spring from the ground to catch her tattered dress, clawing at her bare legs and arms. Her feet were bruised and bleeding from climbing through the forest unprotected. Exhausted, she finally sagged to the ground atop a rocky hillside. She knelt there panting from her exertion, head down and hands limp at her sides, laying against the cool ground. Her matted and tangled hair hung in clumps across her scarred face.

After what seemed like a very long time, she lifted her head, turning her body so she could look back the way she had come. The skyline glowed a dull red above the blackness of the forest across the river. She could hear the water below her, rushing along as though the world were normal. It hissed at her in the dark as if it were a living thing. She sat on the ground, hugging her knees to her thin chest, slowly rocking as tears streaked through the dirt and soot on her young, distorted face.

Fog and smoke swirled and hovered through the trees, enveloping her in their misty shroud. She shuddered, although from cold, fear, pain or exhaustion, it was hard to tell, for they all fought within her tortured mind and body. She let herself drop to the ground in a heap, fighting for sanity, stuffing a fist into her mouth to keep from screaming aloud, wracking sobs becoming occasional hiccups, then quieting to the even breaths of the sleep she feared, yet succumbing to its healing rest, at last.

A full moon finally escaped the clouds and smoke shining eerily behind the fog, lighting patches of forest, then hiding again. A stray, white beam of moonlight finally settled on the young girl as she lay huddled in a ball upon the rocky ground, in fitful sleep, her once raven-colored hair laying in ebony and dirty-white matted strands across her face and neck.

Hours later she awoke to a steamy, misty morning. Gray light filtered through heavy clouds as she watched grotesque shapes become trees and bushes, rocks and sticks. At last she sat up, propping herself on one arm. A chipmunk scurried past her, then stopped, tail raised and flitting. He darted closer to her, then behind a rock, onto the rock, and up the narrow trunk of a sapling. There he peered at her for a moment before darting off again. She smiled thinly, her eyes dull.

As the sun rose higher in the sky, it burned off the fog revealing the damage left by the raging forest fires. Rachel looked at the landscape below her, across the river where all was blackened. She shuddered involuntarily. The Witch had always worn black, even her blood had looked black in the moonlight. Now, the world had turned black too, it seemed.

Rachel slowly brought her hands up and examined them. No, all the black blood had been washed away as she swam in the river. She stared at the trees, seeing nothing. *It's like being baptized all over,* she thought. *All the old is washed away. Now, I'm a new person.* She looked once again at her right hand and arm. Were the scars going away, too? Gingerly, she felt her neck and face with her hands. Her right ear was a knob protruding out of her head. Ridges and seams of injured flesh felt like great hills and gullies. Tears sprang to her good, left eye as she felt the scarred flesh on the right side of her face and head. Her right eye still protruded far out beyond its injured lid. Her hair, once raven black and luxurious, now grew in white clumps between scars on the right side of her head, although the left side was still as fine as it ever was. If she covered her left eye, all she could see was shadow from her damaged right one. The scars were not going away. "I'm not new!" She wailed into the peace of a sunlit morning. Her voice quavered and squeaked. Then she whimpered into her drawn-up knees. "I'm not new. I'm ugly and useless," she whispered hoarsely, sobbing until no more tears would come. Echoes of her tormentor screaming in her face, torturing her with fire and berating her with scriptures of how the wicked would be burned, rang in her head. She covered her head with her arms in an attempt to ward off any more abuse.

When she calmed, she wiped at her eyes and looked once more across the river. Her good eye roved over patches of trees and black stumps, then came to rest upon a grassy knoll. On the hilltop, as though it were shining in the sun, she could see a tiny cabin which hadn't been touched by the fires. She stared hard, trying to see if someone else were alive. "It's my mother's house." She whispered. *Not truly your mother,* came the unbidden thought.

"Yes, my mother." She countered in her croaking whisper. "She sang to me. She told me stories and made things for me." The young woman nodded. "She <u>is</u> my mother."

Rachel Stuart rose up with renewed courage and peered again at the tiny cabin on the hill a few miles away. "I'll go home," she croaked to the house on the hill.

Slowly, for her feet were cracked and tender, she made her way back down the steep mountainside, through the forest to the river. She stood looking at the churning, swirling, muddy water for a long time. Then, mustering what courage she had left, she plunged into its icy embrace, paddling slowly, allowing the current to carry her to a charred meadow on the opposite side. She grabbed at roots and bushes on the bank of the river, slicing her tender hands, but finally able to pull herself onto the sooty, muddy bank and lay there, shivering until at last, she could feel the warmth of the sunshine through her flimsy, wet clothing. As steam rose from her back, she became drowsy and slept until she felt warm and rested.

At long last, Rachel got up and trudged slowly along the wagon track toward the old village. At one sweeping curve, she stopped, staring down the roadway, remembering the bitter struggle for her life only the night before. *Was it only last night?* She cried in fear of the memories as she relived fighting off The Witch. She stared, rooted to the spot until her mind became a void. Then, she turned off onto a narrow path which wound its way up the hills to the tiny cabin. She stood for a moment looking back down at the road, remembering again the events of the night before.

She was free, released at last from her long incarceration, running in the semi-dark, not knowing which way to turn. The Witch grabbed at her in the dark, turning her around with a vicious swat. "You!" The Witch hissed. "No-o-o! The house burns for nothing!" Rachel cowered close to the road, fear and long pent-up venom rising in her heart. "Well, it doesn't matter now," The Witch said in her ugly voice. "Where were you going, I wonder, to see <u>Her</u>?"

"To get away from the fires," Rachel whimpered

in her hoarse whisper, hating the weakness in herself as she groveled before the old woman.

"Liar!" The Witch spat at Rachel. "I know where you were going. But," she laughed a sickening kind of laugh, ugly in its cackling insanity. "She's gone. I killed her, just now, back there in the road." She pointed behind herself with something she carried in her hand. Suddenly, she turned and lunged at Rachel. Rachel knew then that the thing in The Witch's hand was a large knife. Rachel was ready and sidled easily away, grabbing at the wrist of the hand holding the knife. The old woman was no match, even in her madness, for Rachel's youth and desire to live. As Rachel twisted the old claw-like hand, Sarah Stuart seemed to stumble, then fall against the sharp blade. She pulled back, but Rachel's own momentum brought them together again, the blade sinking deep into Sarah's bowels. Rachel screamed and screamed in her squeaky, hoarse voice. Sarah slumped to the ground, never to speak evil or do evil again. Rachel stood looking at what she had done and cried out. "Grandmother, oh Grandmother! Why couldn't you love me? Why couldn't you love anyone?" She knelt there in the road, feeling like she should cry, but no tears would come. She got up and started back to the village, but turned and looked at the black heap in the roadbed. The red glow of the burning village seemed to make the body look deeper black, like a hole or void in the earth with no light. She dragged the old woman's still body to the edge of the road and rolled it down into the ravine alongside. The bushes cracked and broke as the heavy body rolled down the side of the ravine. Rachel ran back toward the village, squealing as loud as she could. "Marianne! Marianne, where are you?" There was no answer and there was no body. She knew then that The Witch had lied again to her.

The entire village was in flames giving an odd red glow to all the black shadows. Rachel ran to her home, but it was engulfed in flames. She put her arms up to shield herself from the heat, then stared at the black stains on her hands and arms. In the eerie shadows created by the burning town, Rachel thought she saw people running for shelter. *Perhaps they're looking for me because of the thing I've done,* she thought. She began to cry, turned around and fled to the river.

Rachel, standing in the sunlit morning, shook the thoughts from her mind. *I'm just like Grandmother,* she thought. *No, it was an accident. She fell on the knife. Yes, but you wanted her dead.* Rachel wiped her hands over her face. It was true. She wished often to be rid of the one who caused herself and so many others such pain. Now, The Witch was dead at her own hand. *But, I only wanted to get away. I never wanted to cause her pain or death. That's the difference between us. I just wanted to get away and find...Find what?*

Rachel was weak and felt overpowering exhaustion, but began plodding on, one foot in front of the other, never looking to the right or left, head down. It was time to leave all the evil behind. She had to look for Mother. The thought that she might not be alone was compelling. But, as she neared the cabin, she could see it was deserted and lonely. Dust and ashes were settling on the table and floor, and complete silence filled the air. No birds were chirping, not even a mouse or a beetle could be seen. *It's just as well,* she thought. She knew everyone thought she was dead. She heard The Witch once telling someone at the door of their house that Rachel had died of some kind of burning fever. *Maybe she was right,* Rachel thought now. *Maybe the old Rachel, the little, tortured girl is dead. There's only me, the 'new' Rachel.* The Witch told them she'd buried Rachel herself, that she had been 'light as a feather' for her. *Besides,* Rachel reminded herself. *Now I'm so hideous no one will want to be near me. I might as well* be *dead.*

Carefully, Rachel moved through the cabin and out the back door into the small garden. She looked at the graves and stifled a sob. One fresh stone caught her attention. The ground didn't look disturbed, but there was a new headstone. She squatted, running a finger over the roughly etched words: 'Marianne Webster Armstrong, died 1694.' Rachel shook her head. *It's only been a few days since I saw Mar-Mother,* she corrected her thinking, *through the cracks in my boarded-up window.* She looked at the other grave markers: *My sister, Amanda, my brother Lucas, my; well, Mother's husband, Will.*

Her good eye narrowed and a crease appeared in the smoothness of her left brow. She stood, frowning down at the ground, then turned and went back into the cabin. Mother's collecting bag was hanging near the door in its usual place. Mother wouldn't leave without her bag. Rachel took it down and put the smaller herb bag into it. She gathered all the food she could find and stuffed it into the big bag. She took a bucket to the well for some water, pumping furiously. She was rewarded for her efforts by a gushing stream of water. She carried the bucket into the cabin, then lighted a fire in the fireplace and started water boiling. She walked out to the barn to see what was left there, but the goat and the horse were gone. Absently, she closed the gates. There would be no milk, but Mother always kept some syrup. That would taste just as good on her corn mush.

After eating, Rachel washed in the basin by the back door. The warm water felt good on her skin. She burned her old, tattered rags in the fireplace after she dressed herself in Mother's clothes. The dress was only a little too big on her. She cinched it to her waist with a piece of Mother's wool string. She spent over an hour combing and cutting tangles from her hair. She parted her ebony hair on the left side and combed it over the sparse, white strands on the right. It felt much better as she ran her hands over her head. For the first time in many weeks, she felt good about herself. She was clean and she hoped her hair looked nice. On an impulse, she took the bucket outside and filled it once again. She set the bucket in the sunlight, then cautiously looked into the water, shining back at her. It was a trick she learned from Mother. If she turned her head slightly to the right, she could see that she didn't look so terrible, but just a little of the right side made her look like a monster. She nearly cried out with the pain of her tortured mind. Instead, she turned her face so only the good side showed and slowed her excited breathing. It calmed her. It was better, much better.

Rachel took the water into the cabin and looked around the inside, then she decided to clean it up for Mother. She washed the dust off everything, sweeping down cobwebs in the corners and finally, scrubbing the floor. As evening drew near she fixed herself some more corn mush and boiled dried meat. The broth and food tasted so good, sliding easily down her parched throat. Until today, she hadn't eaten since...*no, don't think of that!* She reminded herself. *The evil is gone. The Witch is gone. There will be no more pain, no more awful burning of my flesh.* She shuddered at the flood of memories. An image of her head being forced against the hot top of the old wood cook stove caused new tears. She looked absently at her right hand, remembering the searing pain of heat as she pushed herself from the stove, fighting with only her left hand, to get away from The Witch. *'You see!' Shouted The Witch. 'The evil burn and now you know what that means, You Wretched Girl!'*

"*What have I done?*" Rachel had sobbed in her terror and pain.

'*It matters not! You were born to the evil and now your parents have left you to face the punishment of that evil.*' The Witch, Grandmother, had lunged at her again, but Rachel fled into the forest behind the barn.

Rachel picked at the remainder of her food. There was no use fighting the torrential memories. They came unbidden to her tortured mind. Her face softened as she thought of Grandfather finding her in her hiding place and nursing her burns, gently crooning to her in the quiet shelter of the barn. She had never before heard him talk back to Grandmother as he did then. '*Leave this girl alone!*' He yelled at The Witch. '*She's done nothing...*' His voice broke into sobs. '*None of them did anything to you. Now, leave her alone!*'

Tears ran unchecked down Rachel's face as she remembered only a few days later, when she watched as Grandfather fell from the barn loft. '*Get away, you Wretched, Vile Creature!*' Screamed The Witch from the top of the loft ladder.

But, Rachel knelt, cradling Grandfather's bleeding head on her lap in the twilight of the barn. He moaned, but never opened his eyes again. Grandfather, her protector and friend, was gone forever.

Suddenly, The Witch grabbed Rachel by the hair and dragged her into the house. She locked her in the spare bedroom where Mother had been a patient, and boarded up the window. Rachel was never sure how long she was in that darkened room. It might have been only days, perhaps a few weeks. It may have been months, for it seemed like an eternity. Rachel turned pale and listless in her dark confines. She slept much of the time away, unable and unwilling to fight back.

Sometimes The Witch visited Rachel. She read from the old, tattered Bible, always about how the wicked must burn. She brought Rachel a thin gruel and rancid meat to eat. Rachel found beetles in the semi-dark room that, after the first shock of biting into them, weren't so bad to eat and settled the constant pains in her stomach. The Witch often yelled at her and cursed her, berating her with scriptures and lectures as she gave her the minimum of medical treatment. She repeatedly told Rachel how ugly and wretched she looked. She maligned Rachel's parents (her own son and daughter-in-law) who had died years earlier. Rachel withdrew into her own tortured, lonely self. It never occurred to her to yell for help, because she knew The Witch was even more powerful than Father Jonathan. Besides, she didn't want anyone to see her raw, red, and blistered face and head. Even after the physical pains eased from her face, leaving the ridges of scarred flesh, the emotional scarring persecuted her young soul.

One day, The Witch became enraged and yelled, accusing Rachel of talking to others. She slapped her and spat upon her. While she rambled in her rage, Rachel discerned that someone, either Diana or Mother, had asked about her and wanted to see her. Rachel smiled inside, but kept her hope from her face. That glimmer of hope though, filled her heart causing her to peer through the cracks in the boards covering her window and to begin to want to live once again. She couldn't see much from her little peephole, but once in a while, someone passed her sight. She began to wish on every faint star she could see, that she would be rescued. *After all, Brother Will rescued Mother,* she would remind herself. She began dreaming of running free, falling happily into the arms of Mother, or maybe Diana. Still she never yelled out for help as the picture of freedom always faded quickly into another of The Witch dominating her, reminding her of her ugliness and how no one would ever want her now. She wondered time after time why she still lived at all.

As she crouched, trying to see out one day, The Witch came into her room and pounced upon her, choking her and screaming. Rachel fought back, but was no match for the woman who already had a death grip upon her young throat. She felt the snap in her throat and thought she would surely die. The Witch pushed her away and she fell into a crumpled heap on the floor where she lay until darkness enveloped the world. She was never sure when The Witch left her, the pain had so consumed her body and mind until sleep claimed her. Finally, she woke enough to drag herself to the soiled bed. Her throat felt bruised and sore and she couldn't speak or even swallow without pain. Coughing left her in tears and waves of burning, suffering. She drifted in and out of consciousness as time became a meaningless thing. She drank the water from her washing pitcher next to the bed, but only in small sips. Her throat hurt when she attempted to swallow even tiny bits. She was thankful for the thin, tepid gruel provided by her jailor because it went down much easier than would other foods. She learned to let it and the water slide down her throat, swallowing only when she couldn't stop herself.

Slowly, Rachel healed and the pain subsided. But, she was never able to speak again except in a whisper or, when agitated, in a croak or a squeak. It was just one more hideous thing in her hideous life. It left her so that she couldn't yell for help even if she tried. Finally, she desperately wanted to yell. She wondered again why she continued to live.

The Witch is gone, she reminded herself now, shaking off the memories and looking around herself at Mother's cabin. She put down her spoon and looked once again at her hands. The black blood was gone. She pushed away from the table and walked to the door of the cabin. In the last rays of daylight, the river shone like a ribbon laid in the blackened valley. The setting sun softened the effects of the fires.

It confused Rachel to think of the events of the past. She had been able to see so little from her prison room. As she lay on her soiled bed in the little room one evening, only a day or two ago, she had realized the red glow was not a perpetually setting sun, but fire. The forest was burning. She heard folks yelling and got up to peek through between the boards where she saw them running as the fires enveloped the village and threatened everyone. That was the day her tormentor had done little more than push gruel into her room and silently close and lock the door. Rachel listened carefully after she was locked in once again, and thought she heard the outside door close as well. She tried to push the boards off her windows and to open her door, but it took too much strength. Besides, where would she go? No one would want to see her as she was now. She lay on her bed in defeat, and wondering if she would die by fire after all. The Witch always said so. She coughed as smoke seeped into her sanctuary. She thought she could hear flames burning wood. *Maybe The Witch planned this*, she thought. *Maybe she burned down the whole forest and the village and everybody.* She sat up, and as she did so, was reminded of the loose board on the bottom of her bed as it squeaked and rattled under her. She lifted the pallet and pulled the board off the bed frame, then she walked to the door. She tried to open the door again, but it was firmly locked. She slid the end of the board under the door and lifted weakly. Nothing happened, but since she didn't really know what she was doing it didn't surprise her. She tried once more, lifting and pulling at the same time, then lifting and pushing. To her utter amazement, the door popped right open with barely a sound. She fell to her knees as the pressure released, the board clattering on the wooden floor. She sat there staring at the open door in fear for a few seconds, but no one came yelling and threatening her. *The Witch <u>must</u> be gone somewhere*, she thought.

Rachel shook off the memories once again, and sat upon the bench on the porch of Mother's cabin. She breathed deep of the evening air. It still smelled of soot and ashes. She coughed with the effort, her hand automatically going to her throat as though she might protect it against pain. As night fell, she knew that Mother was not going to return to the cabin. Mother was gone. *She had to flee the fires,* Rachel rationalized. Finally, she laid herself on Mother's bed where she slept heavily and soundly through the night.

It rained during the night, lightly at first, then a heavy downpour. Thunder rolled through the valleys, echoing along the roiling river. A light drizzle persisted until the first morning light touched the trees. As the sun rose, so did steam. The sun beat down, radiating on the seared grass and blackened trees. Wisps of fog played among the trees and around the cabin on the hill, playing hide and seek as the sun burned off the moisture.

Rachel stretched mightily, blinking herself awake. A black cat was curled next to her feet. He raised his head to look at her, blinking at her with yellow-green eyes, as she moved around on the narrow cot. "Good morning, Jules," she whispered hoarsely.

"Mew," he answered as he rolled and stretched.

Rachel laughed. Mother's cat would accept her just as Mother would. Unconsciously, her hand moved across the marred and disfigured right side of her head. She got up and rolled the woolen blanket, tying it with a long string that she fitted over her shoulder. She started to pick up Mother's bag when she noticed the red rag on the shelf. She ran her fingers over it lightly. It was Mother's old clothes from her life before she came to the village. She pictured Mother's soft auburn hair and brilliant green eyes. "Where have you gone now?" She whispered, still fingering the old cloth. She thought of the grave in the garden. "No," she smiled sadly. "I know you're aren't dead. You haven't gone there. Someone is playing a little trick."

She laid the cloth back on the shelf and took one more look around the small cabin. She made sure the ashes in the fireplace were cold, then she donned Mother's cloak to cover her head, shouldered her blanket and Mother's bag, and walked out the door, closing it firmly behind her. By the gate, she grasped Mother's walking stick. With a determined smile, she walked slowly down the road toward the old village, the black cat running along behind her.

* * * * * * * * * * * * *

Rachel wandered down the muddy road where steam was rising from pools of standing water, the sun drying the edges of the ruts. She kept her left eye roving, but couldn't see much on her right side. She constantly had to turn her head to the right so she could see a broader view.

She could see before she came to it that the livery stable was burned to the ground. She dug around in the ashes and pulled out some old leather straps and a saddle. The saddle was charred, but usable. There were some hides drying on the fence. She made a pile of the things she thought she might use. Most of the houses in the village were burned, but a shed or two still stood, empty and barren. She wandered around the village ruins looking into every shed and partial building. Someone had been there before her and taken all that was usable. Her own house was burned away and she was glad, for the bad memories were still too new. She could see the cookstove still standing beneath a layer of debris. Rachel looked away. The memories from that place were too dark.

The barn where Grandfather had worked with the wood he loved, was partially standing. She put her bag and blanket on the ground and bent down to go under a beam lying against the still-standing wall. Grandfather's bench was there with some of his tools laying upon it. She smiled as she touched each one, remembering how much Grandfather had loved to make furniture. She could use these things. *It's a gift from Grandfather,* she thought. There was an old pad on a pallet on the floor where Grandfather sometimes slept when he didn't want to disturb anyone in the house. The wind blew and the barn wall creaked causing her to look up at the tangle of partially burned beams and logs. *It might fall on me,* she thought. She turned and ran out under the angled beam into the sunlight, suddenly afraid. *I am alone,* she thought. *I must be careful. Until Mother returns, I must be careful.*

She walked around to the back yard where the root cellar remained untouched. She pulled open the door and looked inside, wrinkling her nose at the musty, earth smell. It was full of preserved food. There were crocks, wooden boxes and barrels of foodstuffs, arranged neatly on the shelves and floor. She closed the door, making a mental note to move Grandfather's cot into the shelter and live there, if she had to. She walked into the remains of the forest behind the barn. It was burned in patches, black and dirty. She picked her way carefully to her favorite tree. The clearing around it was blackened and the tree was smouldering, still. The top of the once magnificent tree was gone, burned away. Rachel walked to the base of the tree. She used the end of Mother's walking stick to poke around at the bottom of the tree, but it was no use, the hiding place was nearly empty. Most of the treasures she kept there were burned. Well, there was the shiny rock and a bone, but everything else was gone. Her feather, her piece of cloth worn by her other mother, they were all gone. The funny little images she had stuffed in there from Mother's locket were gone now, too. "One of them was me." She mused.

Not really you, came the correcting thought.

She shook her head as she looked up at the burned out top of the tree. "It was me." She asserted. "Because Mother gave it to me."

You know that's not how it happened. Her thoughts betrayed her memories.

She shook her head, and as she turned to leave the old tree something shiny caught her eye. There in the charred weeds was a gold button. She smiled and picked it up. It was from Mother's red dress. She clasped the button in her hand and held it close to her heart. *Wherever you are, Mother, I have some of you with me. I won't give up. You didn't, and I won't either. You are alive. I will keep you alive.* She gave one last look at the black forest, then walked away.

The day was growing old and she had much to do. She cleaned off the shelves in the root cellar and brushed away all the cobwebs. She dragged Grandfather's cot into the root cellar and laid it on one of the shelves, then went back into the barn and got his tools and everything that looked useful. She made a space for everything, placing her pack on the shelf above her bed. She reverently laid Mother's blanket on her new bed, smoothing out all the wrinkles, then sitting almost reverently on the bed. *I'll have to be careful not to hit my head on this shelf,* she thought as she touched the upper shelf behind her. She laid down on the bed, then rose, ducking the upper shelf as she sat up. "Meow," asserted Jules as he jumped onto the bed and curled up for a nap. Rachel smiled.

She went back to the livery stable and retrieved the leather and old saddle. *Maybe I will find a horse someday*, she thought as she walked back to her new 'home', dragging her new treasures behind her. She looked at the other homes along the rutted road and noticed a small heating stove standing in a partially burned house. It was still connected to the chimney fashioned by Brother Armstrong. She put the saddle down so she could look more closely at the stove and pipes. She tried to lift the stove, but it was very heavy even though it was small. She finally picked up the saddle and walked back to her cellar where she put her collection on a shelf.

Near the barn were some boards from the fence and a pile of wood Grandfather used to make things. Rachel studied them for a long time. As it was getting dark, she ate some cold food and thought about what she needed to do to survive. She wondered idly where everyone had gone. "Where are Diana and Uncle Edward?" She asked into the gathering darkness. That night, she cried herself to sleep. She was alone, so terribly alone. As though he understood her misery, Jules rubbed against her head, then snuggled close to her as she drifted into troubled sleep.

When morning came, Rachel was up and eating some cold, raw potatoes. She went to the well, but the water wouldn't run. She took an old bucket from the barn and filled it with water from the stream to use in her shelter. Then, she went to work making a sled. When it was finished, it looked crude, but it worked. She put two large, empty crocks on it and went to the stream. There, she used her bucket to fill the crocks. When they were full, she pulled the sled back to her cellar. It was hard, but she could do it. At the side of the root cellar stood an old barrel that had been used for water before. The stone lid stuck out above the root cellar and inside the cellar there was a crude tap near the bottom of the barrel on a shelf close to the door. She used some of the water to clean out the big barrel, then made several trips to fill it up. *I have water inside my house,* she smiled proudly to herself when it was done and she got a drink by turning the tap on the barrel. She wrinkled her nose slightly at the strange taste, but decided it still tasted good enough to drink. "Now, I'll go get my stove, and I can cook too!" Her croaky voice filled the tiny cellar.

She pulled her empty sled down the street and into the yard of the house where she found the stove. She shoved and pulled, and pulled and shoved, and finally got the stove on its side and onto her sled. She put the pipes alongside it. Then the real work began. The sled was so heavy, it kept sinking in the dirt and getting stuck behind clods of dirt or rocks. The pipes fell off over and over, so she gave up and left them alongside the road. When she at last got to her shelter, she realized the stove was too big to put down into the cellar. It seemed so small sitting outside, but she knew it would be too hot in the small space of the cellar. She dumped it off the sled next to the door, and right there, she crumpled into a heap, sobbing tears of frustration and defeat.

When she was emotionally spent, Rachel laid on the ground looking up at the sky. It was past midday already. It had taken her all that time to get this far! As she looked up, her eye was drawn to the remnants of the barn. She sat up and thought, formulating the seed of a plan. *I have some rope and my sled to pull things, even heavy things,* she smiled to herself as she pictured her recent accomplishment. *How can I use those old barn timbers and logs to build a little house?* She looked first at the barn, then at her cellar. *If I can build a room onto the cellar, I can put the stove in it. It won't have to be much, just a little room to live in.* She moaned. She was too tired and sore to work any more today. The sun was shining brightly on her, and as she thought about the project ahead of her, she fell asleep against the grassy side of her cellar.

* * * * * * * * * * * * * *

Thomas Woodslee looked out at the burning forest. From high on his mountain top he could see the forest fires many miles away. His village of people were safe again from the fires that had plagued the vast forests for the past few years. He sighed in relief for his own people even as he wondered about the people who lived in the little village near the river. *These fires must be close to their homes,* he thought. He tightened the saddle on his horse and mounted to ride closer to the fire area. If there were survivors, he would urge them to move into the valley with his own people. It was safer from these fires with its high craggy walls protecting their homes in their wide valley.

Thomas was a young man of about twenty-five summers. He was tall and somewhat gangly, but his shoulders filled out his shirt from his hard work. He wasn't considered handsome, but plain and pleasant looking. He had long, sandy brown hair and brown eyes. His buckskins were too short again. His mother would make him another pair, but he just seemed to grow taller every time she did. *You would think a man of my age would stop growing,* he smiled crookedly as he shook his legs to move his pant legs down over his boots. No one else in their village was as tall as Thomas. He used to be self-conscious about his height, but now he held his head high and walked with pride through the village where he was a skilled tool maker and worked with metals found in the hills. He was well liked and much sought after for his skills.

A few seasons ago, Thomas met Will Armstrong in the forest as they both looked for wood and ore they could work. They exchanged ideas and methods, talking long about their people. Will was older and showed his counterpart some old tricks. Thomas was eager to learn the old ways and to share some of his more contemporary ideas. They talked about the Forbidden Mountains and what lay beyond. Thomas had been even farther than Will and had seen things that scared him. He had retreated to his Hidden Valley village.

"Someday, my people may need yours," Will had said on their last meeting. "Our village grows small. There are not many children, and not many young people to marry and have new ones."

"And someday, we will gladly welcome them," had been Thomas's answer. "How many are there in your village?" He asked in curiosity. "I've noticed it is much smaller than ours."

"There are now under fifty people." Will answered. "We have diminished. When I was a lad, there were three times the number we have now. There have been many deaths and not so many new births."

Now, in light of the recent fires, Thomas went in search of Will Armstrong and his people. Perhaps 'someday' had finally come. He rode carefully through the forest, over one mountain swell and then another. He came to the clearing where Will and others often worked, cutting trees and making building logs. It felt ominous in its stillness. He rode quietly across the clearing, around a pile of logs, and onto the road at the opposite side. He could see it had not been used recently. He walked his horse on toward the old village. As he rounded the last curve in the road, he wasn't surprised by what lay before him. The entire village lay in ruins. Smoke still rose from many stumps and snags, and some buildings. It settled into the valley in grotesque patterns. Thomas dismounted and walked his horse slowly along the mud and dirt road, looking for signs of life. He could see where someone must have survived. Sheds had been emptied and there were tracks in the mud. He found the tracks of a sled with a heavy load. Pipes laying alongside the roadway told that someone must have rescued a stove. He found it laying outside an old root cellar, the stove on its side, the sled sitting near the ruins. Once, he thought he saw movement near the old barn close to the root cellar, but when he studied the scene, there was nothing except a black cat roaming around. He tried to catch the cat, but it hissed and ran into the ruins of the old barn. Thomas laughed aloud. It was an eerie, yet musical sound in the desolation of the fires. It echoed from the burned forest and the shell of the barn. He took a last look around then remounted his horse and rode up the hill to the remote cabins outside the village. "Black." He shook his head. "Nothing but black wherever I look." He settled himself in the saddle and urged his pinto pony forward. Then he laughed ruefully. "Even that cat was black." He glanced back over his shoulder, then rode across the creek and up the hill beyond.

He came first to the Armstrong cabin. He rode slowly around the site, protected from fire by its isolation between the forest and the main village. The buildings were still intact, not even dust had settled inside the cabin. He shook his head sadly when he walked out into the garden and found the grave markers there. His old friend and mentor was gone, then; he and all his family, it seemed. "This is a sad time," he commented, with hat in hand. "Goodbye, My Friend." Then he walked around to the front of the cabin and remounted his horse to ride on. The Macklin cabin was still standing as well, although the barn was partly burned along with some of the fence. The fire had come within fifty feet or so of the cabin. This place too, was deserted.

Thomas turned his horse and rode down the hill through the rocks and brush to the river, south and away from the village ruins. He rode along the river, watching for signs of survivors. He dismounted and walked for a ways when he found where something had been pulled or perhaps lifted itself out of the river. Rain had obliterated most of the evidence, but it seemed to him that someone must have survived. He looked across the river, but was met by silence from the stillness of the deep forest, untouched by the fires. He considered crossing over for a moment, but finally decided to ride along the river toward the rapids and his home in the Hidden Valley.

* * * * * * * * * * * * *

Rachel held very still. She had been gathering boards and had stepped under the leaning beam of the barn to see if she could find anything else to use. She began tying the rope onto a beam to pull it and the remaining pieces of logs across the yard to build her little room onto the cellar. Suddenly, she heard a horse approaching. Her heart leapt at the sound.

Maybe a horse had wandered into the village looking for food and she could catch him! As she rounded the end of the barn ruins, she was shocked to see a man, and he was coming toward her! She shied into the shadows of the ruined building. He kept coming closer and closer. She watched, horrified as he leaned down to pet the cat. Jules didn't like men and hissed as he ran into the barn right to her feet. She grabbed him up into her arms and stood still. The man laughed. It was such an odd sound in her world. She hadn't heard anyone laugh for a very, very long time. Rachel leaned forward to get a better look at the stranger. He was tall and young. She wondered greatly who he might be. She knew he hadn't lived in her village. He was frightening, but the sound of his dying laughter rang like music in her head. She longed to call out, but knew her voice wouldn't work. She also knew he would hate her. Even with her hair combed and her skin washed, she felt ugly now and knew instinctively that she would be loathsome to others. She remained still until he started to ride away. He turned around once more, and she thought he might ride back, so she shrunk back into the corner. But, he righted himself and rode away. She waited a long time after the sound of hoof beats were silent before coming out of the barn.

She never saw the man again, but she thought of him and his laughter a lot. It comforted her when she felt lonely or tired or afraid. Someone was out there; someone kind. A man who could laugh like that must be very kind, she decided. She wished more than once that she had come out of hiding and had talked to him. But, then she would realize that her deformed face and hands and mutilated voice would have driven him away. It was just as well to be alone.

Rachel worked hard at building her little room. She began with a floor. There were ten beams of about the same size. She laid them side by side and pegged them altogether at the ends. Then she built up, one wall at a time. It was hard, back-breaking work for a small girl. The room wasn't as tall on the sides as she had pictured in her mind. She just didn't feel like she could lift the wood any higher than about her neck, she was so tired all the time. So, she made a steep roof on top of it. She made a two-section door like the one that had been on the barn when it was whole. She had enough leather for hinges. She left two holes for windows and made shutters that she could open and close, latching them from inside. She ran up the roadway to retrieve her pipes for the stove. Moving the stove again wasn't nearly as difficult as the first time. It was still heavy, but seemed not so heavy as before. She fitted the pipes into the stove as she had seen it done before. She threw dirt on top of her roof to keep it warm and to help eliminate the danger of sparks from her short chimney. It was done. At last she had a home, and she'd done it herself! Well, mostly herself. The cellar was already done and made up the forth wall of her home. She stuffed the holes where the walls didn't quite meet the cellar with sod from the yard near the burned house, and made some mud and moss stuffing for other cracks and holes. She moved Grandfather's cot out into the room and placed it upon a shelf she had built for her bed. She fashioned a table under one window and used and old stump for a chair. She planned to make a trip up to mother's house with her sled to get the chairs to replace the stump. It had taken her many days, but now it was finished and she felt safe. She could lock herself into her shelter.

As she began her new life, she realized there were many things she needed. She made the long trip up the hill to Mother's cabin and 'borrowed' the dishes, bedding and the two chairs made by Will Armstrong. She took the rest of Mother's clothing along with the wash basin, the tub and scrub boards. When she was finished, the only thing left on the shelves was the tattered, red dress.

With all her acquirements, Rachel's own shelter was now filled and felt like home. She put two down-filled pads on her platform and Mother's blankets, making a cozy and comfortable hideaway.

One still morning, she heard the distinctive ring of axes in the forest beyond the ruined village, and panicked. *The stranger must be coming back!* She thought wildly. She took some food and ran into the forest to hide. But, curiosity got the better of her, curiosity and loneliness. No one came into the village, so she sneaked carefully around the village and into the forest where the men used to cut logs. There she found an old, familiar sight which brought tears to her good eye to see many of the same faces that had worked here before, hard at work once again. She watched and waited, hidden behind a pile of old, cut logs. She truly was not alone, people she knew were close by.

A shadow fell across Rachel and made her jump up. Without thought, she turned to her right, but because of her bad eye couldn't see who was there. She wheeled to her left in panic. Someone started yelling and she heard the pounding of feet. She realized in surprise that she was running into the forest, dodging first one way and then another. She choked back sobs and kept running blindly, falling and getting up and falling again. After a time, she slowed and then stopped, heaving in her exhaustion. There was no pursuit, as she listened intently for awhile. She laid on the coolness of the forest floor, letting her emotions run free, crying for a time then whispering and gesturing, then laying still. Finally, she slept. When she awoke, the sun had moved far to the west. She was in shade and was chilly. She carefully sat up and looked around herself, but no one was there. She listened, but could hear nothing except the beating of her own heart. She had no idea where she was.

Rachel wandered in the forest for two days. She ate what she could find and drank from whatever held water, leaves, old stumps, and depressions in the ground. At last she came to the burned part of the forest, but she had no idea which way she should go. She went down hill simply because it was easier. Just before dark on the evening of the second day, she stumbled into a clearing behind the old church in her burned-out village. She stifled sobs as she ran to her little home where she fell onto her cot and cried until sleep claimed her. There she stayed until morning light.

In the morning, as Rachel lay on her cot, she wondered if the sounds from her own mallet when she was building, had carried out into the forest. She wondered if someone had spied on her as she had on the village men. *Probably not,* she decided. *Someone would have found me by now if they had come looking.* She contemplated for awhile what she wanted to do. She knew now that there were others trying to build a new village down the river somewhere. They wouldn't be coming back to the old village. But, in case someone did, she needed a way to get out of her shelter without using the door. She needed a way to get into the forest where she could hide from them. She wasn't sure why she should hide, but she felt it strongly. For the next few days, she spent her time digging an exit from the back of the cellar. It was hidden inside by the bottom storage shelf. She used leather over a small wooden door to cover the hole of the exit and lined the tunnel with boards and beams. It was more like a series of stairs, which she could crawl out. Then she had to run only a few feet to the shelter of the forest if needed. It gave her comfort to know she could always escape. She practiced over and over until she felt secure. She would never again be a prisoner to anyone. Little did she understand, in her young-old mind, that she would always be a prisoner to herself if she pursued the course she was taking. Every time her heart was clutched in the talons of fear, every time she hid from the outside world, she was locking tighter and tighter the door of her self-made cell.

Two

Fire and Other Terrors

Diana Macklin calmed the frightened horse. "Whoa! Whoa now," she soothed, holding tightly to his mane and patting his neck and chest calmly. "Easy, Boy, be still." The roan gelding finally stood still, though trembling. His eyes rolled back and forth as though looking for an unknown enemy. His ears twitched at the slightest sound, his long tail waving with each movement.

"Again?" Edward Stuart asked softly, as he emerged from the barn. He walked closer to his niece and the frightened horse, adding his gentle touch to calm the frightened animal.

Diana nodded. "Yes, he's here again, and he's more frightened than ever. The goat was with him, too, but I couldn't catch her. She went away off there in the brambles down in the ravine behind the house. She'll come up when she wants to be milked, I guess."

"No sign of Marianne or Will?"

"No," she shook her head, still patting and

soothing the horse. "There's not a mark on him," she commented as she ran her hands over the horse's body. "He's not injured, just scared. The goat looked okay, too. But, I didn't get near enough to her to be certain. I don't know what the problem is. They are scared of something, though."

"Maybe they saw a witch," Edward commented dryly.

"Uncle Edward!" Diana admonished, a look of amusement in her eyes.

"Well, Sarah's been acting that crazy, you know."

"I do know." Diana sighed sadly. "Almost everyone connected to her or at least her home, is dead. All these years, she may have been getting rid of them all."

"Remember how she's always accused everyone else of being a witch?" He asked. "Well, it's because she knew of the evil in her own heart."

"I believe you're right, Uncle." Diana said. "It's a wonder we have survived. Her husband, her children, they're all gone. It was purely a miracle that we got Marianne out of the house alive."

"Is our little Rachel dead then, do you think?" He asked. Pain filled his voice and his face.

He and Diana walked the skittish horse to their corral and turned him loose inside. "I don't know." She finally answered. "Aunt Sarah says Rachel died of a fever..."

"Sarah says!" He spat out in disgust. "Rachel

died just like her parents!" He mimicked Sarah's voice. "Sarah nurses them, and they die." His voice softened. "You nurse them, and they live."

"Like Marianne," she sighed, leaning against the fence. "Although she seemed to heal herself and I was just assisting her."

"And your dear mother," he added.

Diana smiled. "Yes, she was with us a long time after I thought she would go, Uncle Edward. I miss her."

"As do I, as do I.." They stood for a moment in companionable silence. "Martha and Elias both gone and here I linger." Edward mused. "We were the good ones, you know. I don't know how Sarah got to be the way she is." He shook his head in resignation, then brightened just a little as a new line of thought caught his mind. "And now, I miss our sweet Marianne. What do you think is happening over there?"

Diana looked toward the river, but the smokey air kept her from seeing very far. "I suppose we should go over and see. I don't know if Will is back from the fires or not. There's been so little communication. And Marianne has been acting stranger than ever, withdrawing more and more as every one of their children has died. It's like she's here, but not really with us. Oh, I can't explain it. She's always been peculiar. There's been too much to think about and to do with all these fires and people getting burned and dying. You and I haven't had the time to watch out for Marianne, too."

"Well, of course, we've all been busy putting out our own little fires from the debris blowing on the wind. One can hardly think of leaving the house in case it's burned to the ground when you return." Edward was looking beyond their barn, to the west. He shook his head. "These are the worst fires I've ever seen. I think we may need to be prepared to leave. You can almost smell the heat and the burning decay," he nodded as if convincing himself. "It even looks as though the village may be going to be in trouble." He pointed for Diana to see. "The line of fire has gone around these hills, but it seems to be heading right down that little valley where the village is sitting. I hope everyone gets out." They stood again, watching the rising smoke and listening to the crackle of flames beyond their hilltop. Edward looked toward the grave where his sister was buried. "She died in time for us to go, Diana. Your mother wouldn't have been able to last in the wilderness while we wait out these fires. She died just in time."

Diana turned to look at the western mountain tops. "I believe you may be right, Uncle." She mumbled, frowning at the scene before her. "Should we go after that goat?"

Edward shook his head, his white hair waving in the breeze. "She'll come for company once she calms herself on the grass down there. If she sees us leaving, I do believe she'll follow. It's probably why she followed that horse, she didn't want to be left alone."

Diana looked at their modest cottage. "This is the only home I have ever known. I've listened to Marianne's tales and been amazed by her language and the things she always took for granted." She paused in reflection. "Will and some of the others have told tales themselves about what's beyond the Forbidden Mountains. But, this is the only place I've ever wanted to be."

They walked arm-in-arm to the small cottage and sat for a time on the porch. "We've always retreated to the west in times of danger," Edward mused. "But these fires have sneaked around us and blocked that way."

"Why do we always go west?"

"It's the way of safety."

"What's to the East then? If long ago we came from there, what can be so bad about going back that way?"

"I don't know. It's just always been the way."

"Were you and mother born here in this valley?"

"I don't think so. But, like you, it's the only home I've ever known. My father fought Indians and settled here where he felt safety for his young family. I believe Zeb Macklin, your grandfather on your father's side, was a sailor away on the eastern ocean before he found his way here and started raising his family." He waved a hand to indicate a great distance. "There were others, of course. Our village used to be quite large. I never knew my mother's people, but I think they were merchants of some kind. Zeb's wife's people were kind of a wild people."

"Wild, how?"

"Well, they lived away from other folks and gathered herbs and things," he smiled. "Always had goats and sheep. Didn't live right in the village or associate with other folks except to heal and nurture them."

Diana laughed. "Oh, you mean like Mother and myself?" She smiled in return. "Are there others back east?"

He thought for a time. "I don't know, Dear. I truly don't know."

She nodded at his answer and they settled into silence. You could smell the smoke and hear the sound of burning in the forest when all was still.

He smiled at her sadly and said, "We really must go, I think."

She nodded. "Let's go by Marianne's cabin and see if she'll come with us. Will may still be gone fighting the fires, but let's ask her." She shook her head. "I don't think she'll leave."

"Maybe not," he agreed. "She may be safe enough at that cabin. The fires are burning away from the river."

Diana looked beyond their own cabin. "We might be able to stay, too," she said. Then shook her head. "No, let's not take a chance. We can always come back if we want to."

It didn't take them long to gather the meager belongings they would need to survive. They filled their wagon, hitched their horses to it and tied the gelding to the back with their own goat. Diana gathered a few chickens and put them into a woven basket. They boarded the wagon and drove slowly down their dusty lane. As they drove away, they heard the bleat of a goat and the she-goat that had hidden trotted along happily behind their own animals. "She just like to travel," Edward commented dryly. Diana laughed.

The cabin where Marianne lived was empty and sad. They stopped only long enough for Diana to step inside the door and call out. "Marianne!" She called softly, but there was no answer.

As they began their descent into the valley where the village lay, they saw George Bays walking down the road toward the village, a shovel slung over his shoulder, and Edward urged their horses toward him.. "Do you want to ride?" Diana asked as they pulled up alongside of him.

"Many thanks," he smiled grimly and jumped onto the wagon, behind the seat.

"Just back from the fires?" Edward asked.

"Nope," George spat. "Grave digging."

"Who's?" Diana asked, turning to look at him in alarm.

"Brother Armstrong." He said sadly.

"Where's Marianne?" She asked, her voice becoming husky with grief. "We were just there and she's not at home. Do you know where she is?"

"We couldn't get her to leave a day or two ago

when we actually buried Will. She just sat there by the back of the cabin, rocking and crying. When I come up here today, she wasn't anywhere to be seen. I could see where she had been laying on his grave. She slept there, I think, but, now she's gone. I just scratched her out a stone like his." He paused. "I thought maybe she went back where she come from. We don't know where that is, so I just made her a stone, too."

Tears streamed down Diana's face. *Why, oh why didn't I come up here to help her?* She agonized. *Now, Will is gone, and her children. What will become of her? Has she truly disappeared, just like she appeared when she came here?*

"The village is burning," George said calmly, as though he was speaking of the weather. "Most of us are camped in the forest a mile or two up the river. There's not much left of any buildings by today, I reckon."

"Is Rachel there?" Diana asked anxiously. *Maybe Marianne found her way there, too.* She thought.

George frowned. "I thought the girl was dead. Sarah told Father Jonathan she'd buried her."

A frightening picture of Rachel being buried alive came into Diana's mind. She could see her vividly; crying in the dark, alone, frightened, somehow injured. She shook off the image and said. "I know. I just keep hoping she's alive. She's so young. I can't get her out of my mind."

"I thought I saw her once, just before Elias was

killed by that fall. But, when I looked again at the girl I saw in the woods there, behind their place, I couldn't be sure who it was. Might have been Sarah, stooped over, and with her head partially uncovered. Looked older, not so much hair. Rachel always had all that black hair. This person was gray-haired, I think, but she was small like a girl."

They talked then of the fires and of rebuilding. They were quiet as they drove through the town. George was right, it was almost entirely burned. No sounds greeted them. No one walked in the street. It was quiet except for the plodding of their horse's hooves and the creak of the moving wagon. Sarah's house was burned away, with nothing left. The barn was mostly gone, as well. "Heard someone say they saw Sarah torching her own place." George said as they drove past the ruins.

"Why would she do such a thing?" Diana asked.

"I told you earlier she was going crazy. She had a devil abiding with her, maybe for a longer time than we know." Answered her uncle.

"Poor, Rachel. Our poor, poor Rachel!" Mourned Diana. "Marianne and I came down to see about her weeks ago, but Sarah insisted she was dead and gone. Marianne was sure she saw or heard Rachel one day when she was walking past the house. But, Sarah stuck to her story. I guess we'll never know now what happened to her." She cried quietly as they drove on into the forest.

"Well, if Sarah did burn her house herself, I hope Rachel was already dead and buried. I hope she wasn't in that place when it burned." George added with a sad shrug.

They fell into a dread-laden silence that lasted until they arrived, just before nightfall, at the camp. It was a ragtag of tents and lean-to's along the river, in a wide meadow. A hasty corral had been built in the middle of the grassy lea. It was a communal compound for the animals that would keep them mobile and free from hunger while the folks there waited to rebuild their village and could return the animals to their fields.

Diana and her uncle set about putting up a log and sod hut. They slept under the wagon for the first few nights, then were able to move into their one room hut. It was crude, but it was warm and dry. They were under cover just in time. It began to rain harder. Instead of the drizzle and fogs of the past few days, it was a downpour. The sod roof leaked in more than one place, but they were drier than many another family out in the weather.

* * * * * * * * * * * * * *

Frederick Wilder sat in the charred forest and let the rain beat down on him. *Finally, rains heavy enough to put out the fires,* he thought thankfully. He took off his hat and shook the water out, then put it back onto his soaked hair. He ran a hand over his wet face. Then he looked around the steamy, wet forest and nodded in satisfaction. "Well," he said, shouldering his axe and shovel. "I'll go home. The Lord willing, I'll have a home left." He walked down the hill ahead of him into the scorched remains of the once great forest, to the side of a small creek. It was running clear, so he hunched down, scooped out a handful of the cold water, and drank deeply. As he was about to stand, he caught sight of a footprint in the soft mud near the creek. It was a very small footprint, not yet destroyed by the driving rain. He frowned greatly. *A woman! What woman would be out here so far from the village? Why?* He looked down the valley toward his home, still several miles away, then back at the mud. He traced by sight what he thought might be a light trail up the hill to his left. With a sigh, he began following that trail. He saw where the person had fallen, leaving a slight touch of what appeared to be blood on the underside of a leaf. The person had lain quite some time under a patch of brambles and lost a small amount of blood there, too, obviously from a bad injury. The indentation left in the leaves and forest floor was small. *It is a woman!* He thought. *Or a child.* He walked on as far as the ridge of the mountain. There he stood for a long time, just looking out toward the forbidden world beyond the mists. He put down his axe and shovel, wiped his face and head on his sleeve, wrung out his hat, and put it back on his head. *She came, and now she's gone.* He decided. *It's as it should be.*

45

He had been saddened by the death of his friend, Will Armstrong, a few days earlier, but had stayed in the forest to keep a vigil on the fires, while George Bays and his brother had taken Will's body, along with others, back to the village. Now, she, Will's woman, was gone, too. He couldn't tell why, but he was sure it was her. He turned his back and retraced his steps to the creek and on down the steep sides of the valley to his home. The fires had raged through his beloved valley. He came out of the trees slowly, but knew before he got to his own land that his house would be in ruins. Two walls still stood precariously, but they were seared and worthless. His shed was still standing, so he walked to it and opened the door, but all his tools were gone. He shook his head. He had no way of knowing, but hoped his friends and family had moved whatever was left to safety, somewhere. The corral for his horse was busted down, partially burned.

"Been watching for you," came a voice from behind him.

He turned to see his friend, George Bays. "So?" He queried.

"They're all safe up the river a ways."

"Good." He sighed. "For that, I will be forever grateful." He put down his axe and shovel, and was to his friend in two strides. They hugged and pounded each other on the back. "It'll take a lot of rebuilding." He nodded at the village.

"We got a good place where we are. Might think of a fresh start there near the river."

Frederick looked around him. "I lived here near all my life. Don't think I want to move any other place."

"Let's walk," said George. "Then maybe you'll change your thinking."

They walked on the old road along the base of the hills to the river meadow. Frederick surveyed the area, thinking the temporary camp would be in this clearing. "If not here, then where?" He asked his friend.

"Up river a ways," George nodded. "But right now I want to show you something."

They retraced their steps along the road to the edge of a hill. In the ravine near the lane, George pointed. "Look down there."

Frederick looked at his friend, then moved to where he could see over the edge of the ravine. At the bottom was a body clothed all in black. "Is it her, then?" He looked up at George. "The old woman?"

"Yes, it is."

"You been down there?"

George nodded. "She got herself stabbed."

"Murder, you mean?" Frederick frowned. "No one here would do murder. There's never been a murder like that in all my years." He was shaking his head vehemently.

"Maybe she attacked first." George paused. "All I know is, she's dead." He scuffed his toe in the mud of the lane. "That woman of Will Armstrong's is gone. Don't know what's become of her."

Frederick nodded. "She's gone over the Forbidden Ridge."

"So?"

"I saw tracks and followed them. She's gone. I'm convinced it was her." Frederick looked back into the ravine. "How long's the old woman been down there?"

"One, maybe two days."

"It couldn't have been the girl, then. Those tracks were at least four or five days old, I'm thinking. Right about the time you brought Will home."

"Who then?" George asked. "Who would do that?"

"I don't know. The old woman made nothing but enemies." Frederick shook his head in sorrow. Have you told Father Jonathan?"

"Not yet. I been waiting right here, up at Macklin's," he pointed up the hill. "For you."

"Well, let's go tell him and see what he wants to do." He turned to walk away.

"Don't you want to take the body?" George asked.

"No." He paused to look down at the body among the rocks and briars. "I don't want to touch her; not her."

George nodded and turned to stride out alongside Frederick back to the village and on down the road to the camp. It was a joyful reunion with family. They left their news until the following day.

＊ ＊ ＊ ＊ ＊ ＊ ＊ ＊ ＊ ＊ ＊ ＊ ＊

"My, my, my," Father Jonathan clucked his tongue and shook his head slowly. The story he was hearing was the strangest one yet. "When did you say you saw this person?" He asked the young boy sitting across the table from him.

"Yesterday, Sir," the boy answered, encouraged by his father and the attention he was getting.

Frederick Wilder interrupted. "Describe the person again."

"Well, Sir," began the boy. He swallowed hard as he went into a great drama about what he had seen. "Well, I was just walking around. I wasn't doing anything bad or anything like that," he directed at the old monk. "That's when I saw someone coming down the hill from Brother Armstrong's place. It was a woman. She was dressed up and had a pack on her back. Looked like she was going on a trip. But, she had a cloak over her head and I couldn't see her face so good. There was a big black cat following her along the road." He paused and traced a little circle on the table with his finger. "I don't know why I hid. I felt like I was going to get into trouble or something, even though I wasn't doing nothing wrong. I just stepped into the bushes and waited for her to go past me. She turned off just before she got right to where I was. Went down to the old Wit...uh, I mean to Sister Stuart's old place." He looked quickly from one man to the other. "I don't think she saw me hunkered down there in the brambles. She just kept walking. But, what I could see of her face was mean looking! It was all red and ugly! I never saw her before and I don't want to see her again." He took a big breath. "Come to think on it, I don't even know she was real. She might have been a spirit or something. She didn't make no noise that I remember. When she was gone behind the Stuart's barn, I jumped up and ran all the way here."

"Was it Sister Armstrong?" Frederick wanted to know.

"No.....I think she was too small to be her. More like a girl and a woman together."

"Was it Sister Stuart?" Father Jonathan asked.

The boy shook his head firmly. "Nope. She always wears black dresses. This one was dressed in gray or green, like Sister Macklin always wears."

"Was it Diana?" Frederick asked.

"No." The boy shook his head again. "She was ugly, I tell you. Like a...well, like I don't know what. But, she scared me. I won't never go back to that old village. It's haunted or something now."

"Where did she go?"

"I don't know. I just watched until she went around the part of the old barn that's still standing there at the Stuart's place, then, I ran."

"All right. Thank you." Father Jonathan dismissed the boy and his father.

"What do you think?" George Bays asked after a period of silence.

Father Jonathan stood and walked to the flap of his spacious tent. "I don't know. It couldn't have been Sarah Stuart. She's been dead too long down there in that ravine. That must have happened on the first night of the village fires. Frederick, here says it can't have been Marianne Armstrong because she's gone over the mountains. The Macklin's have been here for several days."

"Who, then, a ghost?"

"Ah-h-h-h!" Frederick slapped the table, causing the others to jump. "That boy's just lying to cover up that he was cleaning out all the buildings in the village. He doesn't want to get caught and whipped by his father."

Father Jonathan smiled. He was looking out over the makeshift camp. *Perhaps Frederick was right. The boy could be lying.* He considered his tiny flock as they went about their early morning chores. There were so few left, maybe twenty or so men, most of them with wives, and about eight children, two girls and six boys. *Where have they all gone?* He brooded. *There used to be a busy, full village and now I'm left with these few. There's barely a future.*

Cooking fires were burning in front of the crude huts and tents and wagons. Men were tending the animals in the fenced center circle of the camp. He heard an axe or two out in the forest. *But, life goes on,* he thought. *We'll rebuild, and life will just go on as it always has.* His thoughts moved to the time when Will Armstrong brought the strange girl out of the mountains. *Nothing has been the same since that time.* He reminded himself. *Now, after so many years, the village is gone and we must start anew.* He smiled again. It would be good to start again. *But, there are so few people left, and even fewer children.* He shook his head. *What will we do with so few of us to go on?*

"We sent some fellows out to bury Sarah," Frederick was saying. "I told them to just put her in the ground right where she was. Do you want a cross or marker or something?"

Father Jonathan nodded absently. He thought of the years of tyranny by that old woman. She had run everything. *Even me,* he remembered with chagrin. He looked down at his feet. *It will be different now. I can actually lead this people. I won't have to appease a bitter old woman. The unexplained deaths and illnesses will cease.* He closed his eyes. *I looked away. I never confronted her. I just looked the other way when 'things' happened.* He let his mind rove over the last thirty years. *"My daughter is evil." Old Sister Elizabeth Macklin had confessed on her deathbed. Granted, she was odd and overbearing, but evil?* It took him years to learn the hard truth. Even now it seemed impossible. *How many deaths?* He asked himself.

Her own mother? Surely not! But, he could never be sure. James Macklin, Sarah's brother and husband of Martha Stuart, died in a hunting accident. At least that one couldn't be attributed to Sarah. She surely wouldn't have gone out in the woods and shot her brother to death. *No, it seems to have started with her son. She never wanted that boy to marry. It galled her that he did it anyway.* He thought of young Elijah Stuart, robust and happy. He was a strapping lad, handsome and caring. He had much of his father's compassion in him. He married the beautiful Ruth Smith and they made such a lovely, happy couple. Everyone except Sarah was so excited when they gave birth to Rachel. Sarah had raged as usual. She insisted that they live in her own house. As much as she seemed to hate Ruth, she still wanted them to live with her. Sarah would never let anyone see the couple once they took ill. Then, they were dead and buried. Elijah, then Ruth, that fast. *How did Rachel ever escape?* He wondered. A shiver of premonition shook him. *Poor, poor Rachel. She finally succumbed to death as well, so Sarah said.* He shook off the images of Rachel hiding in the barn, her grandfather caring for her, lying to protect her. How many times? Now, Elias was dead, too. Quiet, thoughtful Elias fell from the barn loft, Sarah told them all. *And what about that mysterious fire at the old mill?* He asked himself. Ruth Smith's parents had died in that fire. They never even got out of their beds, just burned up in their sleep. *"Sarah Stuart has killed our daughter and her own son,"* Sister Smith *confessed to me that day in the church,* he remembered. *"She starved them or gave them something that made them sick. I don't know what, but we're going to take that baby and raise her. She'll never know love in that house."* And then, they died. *Surely Sarah didn't do that, too.* He frowned at the ground. He had no proof of any of this. But, his heart knew, his heart knew and it made him sick to think of his own part in these deaths. He did nothing. Did that make him a part? Even years later, it had been so easy to blame all the strange happenings on the mysterious Marianne brought to them by Will Armstrong when they really had their own fearful mystery among them.

"Father?" George Bays laid a friendly hand on the monk's shoulder. "Is there anything else you want us to do?"

He shook his big head. "No, no, we've done all we can. Well, maybe go to the village and have a look around, see if we can go back and rebuild there."

"Brother Wilder and I will look around there, if you like." He said.

"Thank you. You are good men." The old monk smiled. With men like these, he could build a good community, a better one than they had before. But, they would have no blacksmith, no tool and furniture maker, no miller.

Frederick and George didn't go back to the village.

They knew there was nothing there. The work sheds had been cleaned out by others. Once Sarah Stuart was accounted for and Diana and Edward had ridden in, there was nothing left for them to worry about, everyone else was dead or gone. It was time to start fresh. They gathered some of the men and boys around and began work in the logging clearing, cutting new timbers. No matter where Father Jonathan decided to settle them, they would need building materials.

On their second cutting trip, one of the boys, a lad of about twelve seasons, encountered something strange in the forest. "Ah-h-h-h-h!" He came running to his father, screaming at the top of his lungs. It took some minutes to calm him down enough to speak. "A witch! There was a witch over there!" He gestured wildly in the direction from which he had come.

"What do you mean, a witch?" Frederick tried to ask calmly. He felt the prickle of foreboding along the back of his neck.

Others began to murmur. "We should have burned Old Sarah's body," someone said in a loud whisper. Frederick looked around the group, but couldn't tell who had been talking.

The boy had picked up his story. "I was just walking over there." Again the vague gesture. "I saw somebody hunkered down by a tree. It wasn't one of us, so I went up to see who she was."

Frederick broke in. "She? It was a woman?"

The boy nodded vigorously. "A little, tiny woman."

He affirmed. "She turned on me as I came up to her and, and," he ran a hand over his sweating face. "It was awful!"

"What?!" Frederick nearly screamed at him. "What was awful?"

The boy jumped back toward his father at this new threat. He trembled and began to cry.

George laid a calming hand on his friend's shoulder. "Tell us in your own time, Boy." He soothed.

The boy's father nodded his thanks. Finally, the boy calmed down and began again.

"She, she had ugly, lumpy skin and her eye," he paused and shuddered. "It was kind of hanging out of the hole." He shook his head and closed his eyes at the memory. "She jumped up out of the bushes and turned toward me. She didn't have any hair, just a black shawl over her head. She hissed and gagged at me. Then she shrieked and I turned tail and ran as fast as I could back here." He sagged against his father. "Didn't anybody else hear her shriek like that?" He looked at his father.

"No, Son," his father soothed. "We only heard you screaming as you ran into camp."

"What do you think?" George asked his friend.

"I don't know." Frederick shook his head in amazement. "I don't believe in ghosts." He stated, looking a challenge around the group.

"What happened to that woman of Will

Armstrong's?" Someone asked. Others nodded and murmured in agreement.

"She's gone!" Snapped Frederick. He stared hard at the group. Then his face softened as he looked at his friend. "George, let's see what's over there."

They walked slowly into the forest. What they saw did nothing to allay their fears, but it did perplex them. Huddled under some brush was a big, black cat. As they approached, the cat jumped up, hissed, spat at them and ran up a tree. Frederick took off his hat and scratched his head. George rubbed his hand over his new beard.

"The boy would have known a cat, wouldn't he?" Frederick asked.

"He was scared," answered George.

"But, a cat doesn't look like a woman..." Frederick looked up the tree where the cat had run. He moved around the tree. "Now, where did that cat go?"

George moved around the tree, too. The cat was nowhere to be found. He shook his head. "You don't think..."

"No, I don't!" Frederick growled. "And you shouldn't either!"

"I know," said George. "But, uh, where's the cat?"

They both continued to look until it became apparent that they were not going to find it. Frederick looked at the ground. "You know," he reflected. "Someone could have been sitting here." He indicated a spot where the grass was matted down. "Something heavier than a cat made that depression."

They looked around some more. They could see plainly where the boy had stood, then spun around and run. The dirt and weeds were scuffed. They could also see where someone else might have done the same thing, but running in the opposite direction, into the forest. But, the step was so light, they couldn't be sure. They didn't pursue it, just retreated to rejoin their friends. "Nothing, just a black cat and nothing else," George answered when others questioned him about what they'd found. Neither of them elaborated on the cat. There was no need in fueling thoughts of witches with sightings of black cats.

"Will Armstrong had a black cat," someone offered in explanation, and that seemed to settle the matter.

Later that night, they sat with Father Jonathan long after most others had gone to sleep. "A black cat. A black shawl. Could he have mistaken the cat in his fear and made up the rest?" Father Jonathan asked.

"It's possible," answered George. "But it did look like someone may have run off into the forest." He shook his head. "I just don't know."

"It would be possible if it was the only account of some mysterious girl/woman with a black cat." Stated the monk. He sighed deeply, staring into the dying flames of his fire. "Will this people never be free of witch stories and mysterious women?"

The men of the displaced village were now reluctant to cut more than firewood or to rebuild their homes, even new ones along the river if they had to be so close to the old village. Stories were running rampant among the children who were afraid to gather firewood and had trouble going to sleep at night.

* * * * * * * * * * * * * * *

The day the stranger appeared you could feel the fear like a palpable thing. He rode his horse slowly into the make-shift camp, coming along the river from the direction of the old village. Frederick recognized the young man and stepped out of the staring crowd to greet him. "Thomas," he nodded.

"Hello, Frederick." The young man dismounted and stretched his back. "I've been looking for survivors." He indicated the group behind Frederick. "Is this all?"

Frederick turned to look at the small group behind him. "Yes," he said sadly, turning back to Thomas. "We're all that's left."

Thomas nodded. He removed his hat to smooth down his hair. "What plans have you? Are you going to rebuild?"

"We've been talking about it, but progress has been slow."

"I went up past Will's place. I'm sorry to hear about him and his family. He was a good man."

"Yes, we'll miss him."

"He told me one time, you might need some help someday. I'm here to offer what I can."

"Trouble is, we can't decide what to do. Come and sit, and we'll talk about it." Frederick led Thomas to the tent where he was staying. They made room at the table and the village men gathered around to hear what would be decided. Diana Macklin joined them, standing at the back of the tent, near her uncle.

"I speak for the whole community when I say you are welcome to join us. I talked with the elders before leaving home and they were going to begin clearing a section for new houses. They may even have begun to build three or four modest cabins. We weren't sure how many folks I might find, if anyone at all."

"You mean leave the valley altogether and live with others?" One man asked.

Frederick lost his temper. He had listened for days about the fears of living in this valley. Now, with the opportunity to move, he was hearing complaints about doing that! "You can't have it both ways, John!" He growled at the speaker. "You're afraid to go and afraid to stay here, too."

"Afraid?" Asked Thomas.

"There's a ghost-witch in the forest." The man named John answered. "My boy seen her."

"Mine did, too!" Added another man.

Thomas raised his eyebrows at Frederick. "A ghost-witch?" He asked skeptically. He could barely keep from smiling. *Surely they're not serious*, he thought.

Frederick shook his head in disgust, but it was

George Bays who answered. "We're not sure what the boys saw. We looked ourselves, but only saw a black cat."

"A big cat that hisses at you?" Thomas asked.

"Yes," George nodded in agreement. "It went up a tree and then disappeared before we saw where it ran to."

"That's because it was a ghost," explained John.

"Bah!" Exclaimed Frederick.

"I saw a black cat like that in the village a day or two ago when I rode through. I think it's living in the ruins of an old barn at the far end of the village."

"You see? That's old Sarah's place!" John said as though he'd just explained it all.

"You can see what we're dealing with, " apologized Father Jonathan.

Thomas laughed merrily. "I can." There was a lot of muttering and talking around the table for a few moments. "I truly mean to take you folks and your belongings back home with me." Thomas said into the muttering.

George looked keenly at him. "How far away are we talking?"

"Only a few days with wagons, maybe three or four."

"You're sure your village wants all of us?"

"We have plenty of room in our own valley. We aren't surrounded by the forest as you are, but by mountain walls, so the threat of fire isn't so great. It's a long, green valley with plenty of graze for the animals and room for all of you."

"It shouldn't take us long to get ready to travel." Father Jonathan looked askance of Frederick.

"No, we could all be ready in just a few hours. Is it what we want to do then?" He looked around at the quiet group.

Diana spoke for the first time. "I have never lived anywhere but here. I would like a few days, maybe one or two, to just get used to the idea, and to say good bye." She bowed her head slightly. "My mother is buried up on the hill."

"Purely a woman's way of thinking," said Thomas as he appraised Diana. "And purely acceptable. I am in no hurry."

Diana blushed at the attention, but thanked Thomas for his kindness. "Do you have a healer in your village?" She asked.

Thomas looked at Diana with renewed interest. "Yes, we do. We have two, rather elderly women, who take care of us. You, if that is your calling, will be a welcome addition."

"Thank you," Diana said meekly, as she slid an arm around her uncle.

"It sounds too good to be true, doesn't it?" He asked her.

"I've heard Will speak of these people." She answered. "He had nothing but good to say. I think it's the answer."

"I often wondered if it were a little fantasy of Will's from so much time spent beyond the forbidden mountains and the hidden forests across the river." Edward admitted. "It was a nice fantasy that kind of contradicted the gloom and doom Sarah always spouted."

"And they come from the east, Uncle. Perhaps they are all long, lost relatives and we are about to go back to our roots."

"Perhaps, Dear, perhaps." Edward patted her hand.

George Bays suggested to Uncle Edward that if he and Diana wanted anything from their old home they should go there by way of the river path up past Armstrong's cabin, and not go through the old village. "If there is some kind of evil presence, it hasn't been seen up on the open hills." He said. "There's no use in taking chances that some force means harm to us."

Diana was ready to scoff at the idea, but saw the earnestness in George's eyes and knew him to be a kindly man. She felt his concern and both she and Edward thanked him. "I'll go on horseback," she said. "And I'll stop by Marianne's to get their carriage. They won't be needing it and it will be large enough to get what little we left behind."

"No! Don't go alone!" Uncle Edward said. "I'll go with you. Please, don't go alone."

So it was, that Edward and Diana rode back to their old home. Diana rode slowly along the river, stopping often to look at plants, picking a few to add to her bag, and seeing to it that Uncle Edward was well rested. Even though it was only a very few miles to the Armstrong cabin, it took them until well past midday. "I'll fix us a meal and we'll rest the horses here before I hitch Jim up to the carriage." She said. They turned both horses out into Marianne's small pasture to graze while they went inside the cabin. Diana was surprised and curious to find the cabin clean. *Odd,* she thought. *It's almost as if Marianne had just been here.*

The two chairs which normally sat at the table were gone, so Diana and her uncle sat on the bench on the porch to eat their picnic lunch. "Someone's already started stripping this place down," she commented. "I wonder who?"

"I wonder, myself." Answered her uncle. "Someone who needs a little comfort, I guess."

"Yes, but..." Diana never finished. A thought came to her and she walked back into the cabin to take a better look around. She returned to the porch more perplexed than ever.

Edward looked up at his niece. "Well?" He queried.

She frowned in perplexity as she sat next to him on the bench. "The bedding is gone, the dishes are gone, Marianne's personal things, her herb bag and clothes, are gone. Neither Will's nor the children's things have been touched. They are covered with dust and debris while the rest of the cabin is much cleaner. I don't know what to think of this."

"Is she alive somewhere, do you think?"

"Who, Marianne?" Diana shook her head slowly. "No, at least not here. Frederick is sure she walked over the mountains and away. She couldn't have carried all this stuff with her."

"Perhaps she's come back." Edward offered.

"I don't think so, Uncle. I believe this has something to do with our mysterious 'woman or girl in black' the children have been seeing."

"Perhaps the boys are playing a trick on the fathers. Perhaps they have taken these things and made a little fort for themselves."

"You may be right," she agreed. "Well, let's hitch up the horse and see what's left at our own place. Maybe it's been cleaned out, too and we have made this trip for nothing."

They arrived at their own home well before nightfall, but decided to stay and spend the night. Nothing had been touched. It was just as they had left it. Diana packed up all the things she'd left behind in a hurry, leaving only those things they could make again. Edward insisted on tying the rocking chair he'd made for his sister to the back of the carriage. "We'll need both horses to pull this carriage if we put much more in it," she chided.

"Ah, but let's be comfortable, shall we? In our new home, I mean. I'm too old to be building much new furniture, and while they might have great craftsmen, I'm used to this old chair. It's like taking a piece of your mother with us."

65

Diana hugged him. "You're right, of course," she said.

They retired early, Uncle Edward sleeping in the bed that had been his sister's and Diana sleeping on bedding laid on the floor. Then, they made an early start in the morning. It was barely daylight when they tied the last of the bedding and clothes onto the carriage and drove away. Diana did not look back, but forward to the new life she hoped was to be hers.

"Where are you going?" Uncle Edward asked when she turned the horse down the hill.

"Through the village." She answered in determination. "It's much faster, and I want to see something."

Edward Stuart knew better than to try to dissuade his niece once her mind was made up. He rode along silently, saying a little prayer for safety.

They drove slowly through the village. Diana stopped at the corner of the main street contemplating the silence of the deserted village. Her mind made up, she turned the horse to the left and drove to the end of the street where it crossed the creek and became a muddy track into the forest. She turned the horse around, peering closely at the old home of Sarah Stuart as she passed. She paused in the semi-darkness. "See?" She whispered to her uncle. "Those boys have built themselves a little play fort right there by the old root cellar."

Uncle Edward nodded. They had indeed. It was

crude, but good enough to play in. "Those little scamps!" He chuckled. "They made up those stories to keep the adults away."

"Yes," she mused. "Then why are we whispering?"

Uncle Edward shrugged. "It seems appropriate in this still morning air," he answered.

"Years in this village with Aunt Sarah has made us all a little crazy, I think." Diana said in a low voice. "Come on, Jim." She said aloud, clucking to the horse and jiggling the reins. She trotted him quickly to the east end of the village and on to the camp where they would gather their household and animals for the long trip to their new home. Again, Diana never looked back. Her future was forward. But, if she had, she might have stopped and reconsidered.

* * * * * * * * * * * * * *

Rachel awoke with a start. She heard the unmistakable sounds of a horse and wagon or carriage. It stopped on the road only feet from her crude cabin. She cowered in fear as it sat there for what seemed like a very long time. Carefully, she crept from her bed and opened the door to her escape tunnel, then scurried through, being sure to close the door behind her. Once in the trees, she peered into the mist of early morning at the carriage on the road. It looked like two people, but she couldn't be sure. Her vision was blurry from sleep and the disadvantage of having only one good eye.

Rachel heard the melody of Diana's voice as clearly as the beating of her own heart. 'Come on, Jim', it said. Then the carriage was moving swiftly away. Rachel ran to the road, her voice croaking and hoarse, but a whisper still. "Diana!" she called. "Diana!" But, the carriage soon disappeared around the bend in the road at the far end of the village. The two people in it never looked around to see the pathetic figure prostrate on the ground behind them, pounding the earth and crying in the morning light. Rachel sat up on her knees with her hands in the air. "Di- an-n-n-n -a-a-a!" She shrieked. The eerie sound squeaked and trilled among the trees close to the village.

In the dimness of the forest, Diana brought the horse to a stop in the road. "Did you hear that?" She asked, looking back the way they had come.

"It sounded like a hurt animal, maybe a rabbit." He answered. "Did we run over some poor little thing?"

"No," Diana said, worry etched in her face. "No, I thought I heard my name on the wind." They sat still for a few moments, but heard nothing more. The trees stood silent, no breeze was blowing to stir their branches. Diana felt a chill. "There's something..." she said. She hesitated, looking back toward the village. Finally, when no other sounds could be heard, Diana sighed. "Come on, Jim." She flicked the reins along his back..The horse moved forward.

Three

The Land of Fog and Mist

"This is crazy, William!" Anita complained. "We are going around in circles following her."

"If we could actually ever catch up to her, it would help." William grumbled into the small fire they'd built against the chill of another night in the damp forest. "Is there any food at all?"

"No, but I'm sure she'll leave us another tasty morsel in the night." Anita grumbled back. They fell into silence, each staring into the flames of their small fire. "William," Anita said. "I am going back." He looked at her dully. "One of us has to get some help. Whoever she is," Anita waved vaguely at the forest. "She is in more mental distress than we thought. I know I'm out of my element and in way over my head."

"You're probably right," he said in a tired voice. He rubbed his hand over his unshaven jaw.

"Are you going to be all right to stay with her? It may take me several days to get anyone back up here."

"Hm," he grunted. "What I need is a good night's sleep, and to be dry. I'm sick of this wet, foggy weather." He broke into a ragged cough.

"I know," she answered when he had quieted. "I don't think it's natural. The fog, I mean." She shuddered. "I don't know. I feel like we're in some kind of dream that belongs to someone else. It's like a time warp or something. Oh, it sounds crazy to put my thoughts into words!"

"It's true, though." William said quietly. "I think the same way. It's as if we haven't progressed past the first day, yet we keep walking and walking." He coughed again. "Day and night, come and go. You're right. It is crazy. We are in some kind of crazy fantasy of her making." he waved weakly at the forest.

They were quiet for a few moments, reflecting on the things they had just said. It couldn't be explained with any kind of logic. They were embroiled in someone else's madness, or a nightmare, *or the Twilight Zone,* thought Anita. *One of us has got to gather together some kind of sanity and walk away from this <u>insanity</u>.* She looked across the fire at William who was sitting lethargically with his head down, his hands hanging limp from arms resting on his drawn-up knees. "Are you okay? Is your fever back?" She asked with concern. He looked so pale.

"I'm okay." He mumbled, suppressing a cough. "I'm just so tired. I'm tired of all this wandering, and rain, and fog, and the illusive Mrs. Armstrong!" He smiled sardonically. "Is she even real?" He asked with a crooked smile.

"That is a question, isn't it?" She answered. "However, you are, and you're looking pale again. Is your fever up?"

"Perhaps a little," he admitted. "I just need to rest, I think, really rest, not these cat-naps I've been taking, and not out here in this constant wet weather."

"Well, you can't go getting pneumonia or anything like that, William," she admonished. "Especially if I'm going to leave you here all alone." She stared at him for a moment. "Maybe we should just go back and leave her out here. She's perfectly adapted to it. I could help you walk out of here."

"How would we explain that?" He asked. "We take a patient on a trip then come back without her. No trace." A wracking cough overtook him.

She put her hands on her face and sighed. "Oh, I don't know. Who's idea was this trip, anyway?" She laughed without humor. It had seemed like the perfect way to get Marianne Armstrong or Julie Kincaid, whichever one the girl was, to face reality, accept her life, and go home to her family. Anita had felt a camping trip out here where Marianne had been found would lift her amnesia and help her. It would be fun to camp and get away from the rat-race of their work at the hospital, she'd explained to William to convince him to come on this trip. Now, look what had happened. The first morning, Marianne had taken off into the fog, just keeping in sight, waving them on and on and on. "How long have we been out here?" She mumbled to herself. "One day? Two? Ten?" She shook her head in weariness.

"Will you be okay?" William asked, breaking into her reverie.

"I think so," she nodded. "I can follow the pieces of rope we tied to bushes. That should lead me near the campsite. From there, I can follow the road back to civilization. I can't believe no one has been out here looking for us."

"How long have we been out here?"

"I'm not sure. I was just asking myself the same question. Three days? Maybe it's been three weeks or three months. What do you think?"

"I don't know, either. Time doesn't seem to mean the same thing here as it did before." He paused, breathing shallowly, fighting every moment not to cough. *I'm really not well,* he thought. *Anita's right. She's our best hope of getting home.* "I think it's only been a few days." He said. "The last time we were up that hill, he indicated somewhere behind Anita. " I could still see the car down below, so this is only the second time we've been this close. Let's see, about six days, maybe, I think this is the fifth night, if day and night mean anything now." He stopped for a coughing spell and to catch his breath. "You won't need the markers, it's just over the hill there behind you, I'm sure of it." He began coughing again.

"She's been taking down the markers anyway," Anita commented. "I'm glad we're this close, though." She thought for a moment. "It sure agitated her to find out we'd been marking the way." She pictured the confrontation on the day when Marianne noticed the rope markers. Anita had tried to get Marianne to go back to the car so she could get more medication for William. She was worried he was getting pneumonia. *'Look, Marianne,' she'd said on one of the rare occasions when Marianne came close enough to communicate with her. 'We're going around in circles. We need to go home, now.' Anita showed the pieces of rope tied to bushes and trees as trail markers, to Marianne.*

'What have you done?' Marianne asked. 'No wonder we can't get to the village! You've been drawing us back into your world all along!' Marianne stomped off into the forest for a long time while Anita nursed a very sick William Avery. He had roused himself the next day and they journeyed on, hoping Marianne was leading them back to their campsite. That was two days ago, Anita thought now. "She might have brought us this close to the car on purpose," Anita mused. "Perhaps she wants me to go for help. In some twisted way, she might understand how sick she is."

"Leave at first light," William said. "I'll keep her right here, if I can. I'm not feeling too well, so maybe she'll stay here with me if you're gone."

"Or just drop you off some more herbs like last time."

"You won't be here, so maybe she'll actually help me. I might get a chance to talk to her."

"At least it isn't raining anymore." Anita said on a brighter note.

"Yes, I'm finally feeling dry around the edges."

"How are your feet?"

"Oh, their fine. My feet never got wet, just tired. Are you okay?"

"Yes, my shoes have kept my feet dry, too."

Their conversation died of its own weight, as they prepared for another night in the wilderness. William spread dirt on the small fire as Anita made their semi-dry beds. They were asleep in minutes under a rough lean-to of cedar branches. For the first time in days, the clouds dispersed and the moon shone down in its silvery splendor. An owl hooted as it flew through the clearing where they'd made camp.

Anita awoke early, completely surprised to find Marianne sitting in their camp. She had a fire going and was warming some water. The pungent odor of steeping herbs permeated the camp. Marianne nodded toward William, asleep in his single blanket. "He's sick again."

"Yes, he is," answered Anita. "I need to go for help."

Marianne seemed to consider what Anita said. She looked from one to the other of the people she had been leading through the forest. Slowly, she nodded. "I see the wisdom in your leaving us," she said quietly.

Anita was so relieved. She had feared that Marianne might try to keep her from going. But, it appeared that Marianne would let her go get help. Right away she began gathering her meager belongings together. "Thank you," she breathed. "Thank you, so much! I'll be back soon, within a few days. Just sit still right here, I'll be back with help, I promise. I'll leave you my sleeping bag to keep William extra warm." Marianne stood as Anita approached her. Awkwardly, Anita gathered the girl in her arms and hugged her. "It will be all right, I promise," she whispered.

Marianne nodded. "I know," she whispered back. "I know it will."

Anita started out at a brisk pace. She was excited at the prospect of being back in civilization, of getting help for them and their crazed charge. "It will be all right, now!" She muttered to herself as she climbed the craggy hill. From the top, she could see their former campsite. The car was gone, but that was okay. It meant someone had been looking for them and would probably be back. She looked once more at the camp where she'd left William and Marianne, but it was already entirely shrouded in a wayward wisp of fog. "Strange how that fog wafts around everything," she murmured. "It moves around like it has life all of its own." On top of the hill, the sun was shining brightly, yet William and Marianne were hidden from her less than a half mile away. Doubt seized her for a moment. *Maybe I shouldn't leave him,* she thought. *What if I never see him again?* She shook off the gloomy thoughts. *What am I thinking? It's our only hope! I'm our only hope!* She looked at the foggy forest once more. "Good-bye, William." She said. "I'll be back as soon as I can, if I can." She sighed. "Someone will be back for you. Someone will." With that, she walked down the mountain to the old campsite, then on down the narrow road toward civilization.

* * * * * * * * * * * * * *

Marianne tried to nurse William back to health, but he wasn't responding to her medicines. "I'm just not as good at this as Diana," she mumbled. She bathed him once again in warm water and forced a few spoonsful of tea into his mouth. He roused for awhile to drink some broth and nibble at a grass seed cake she made for him. "I'm going to take you to Diana," she told him. "She'll know what to do."

"Who's Diana?" He asked in a hoarse whisper, with no real interest.

"A friend."

"Why haven't we seen her before now? We've been wandering lost out here for days..." He was stopped by a coughing spasm.

Marianne wagged a finger at him. "You and your nurse were naughty," she said as a mother might chide an errant child. "You left markers that tied us to the outside world."

William stared at her, too sick to protest, but wondering and worrying about what she might have in mind now that Anita was gone.

"Do you think you can walk again?" She asked.

"No." He shook his head with emphasis.

"Okay. I'll be gone for a little while to make a travois. Just rest here, I won't be too long."

William laid back and closed his eyes. "Let's just stay here, okay?" He asked weakly. "Anita will be back soon and I'll be better. Then we'll go for a walk, I promise."

Marianne smiled at him with pity in her eyes. She let him drift into a fitful sleep, then walked into the forest to find the supplies she would need. She was back in only a few moments. She used his blanket on the poles she'd gotten and grapevines for braces and a pulling 'rope'.

"Marianne, please wait for Anita to return," William pleaded with her as she fitted him onto the makeshift bed. "I'll go with you on my own two feet by the time she returns. Let's wait, shall we?" He knew it was in vain, and he knew he didn't have the strength to stop her. *Well,* he thought. *Maybe there really are people out here somewhere and we can find them. Maybe she really does know where she's going. Maybe, maybe....*

Marianne pulled the travois over the rocky, log-strewn forest floor with some difficulty. It wasn't easy to pull such a heavy man over rough terrain. But, he was lighter than she'd thought he would be. It wasn't impossible. She turned her back on the hill where Anita had disappeared and went what she hoped was straight away to the east and south, over one mountain ridge, then over another. The traveling was easier where the forest had burned. The ends of the sticks didn't dig into the soft mud and dirt too much, so it slid quite nicely.

Marianne looked for landmarks, but she couldn't see anything she recognized. Everything looked the same, forward, backward, to her left and to her right. On the afternoon of the second day, she thought she could see just a fringe of green over the hill before her and made her way toward that. As she topped the hill, she beheld the vast damage of the fires. She knew she was on the ridge of the Forbidden Hills. It was higher than all the others had been. The green fringe of trees was still a hill or two away. To her delight, there was a stream at the bottom of this hill. She would make camp there for the night. As she looked behind her, she was equally happy to see the obscuring fog closing in behind them. It was a good omen. She would be home soon. *Home, whatever that means for me,* she thought. But, she smiled contentedly, none the less.

The night was uneventful. Will, as she insisted on calling William Avery, was responding to her potions and herb treatments. His coughing had abated to occasional spasms, but he was still wracked with a high fever from time to time. "I think I could walk for awhile in the morning," he commented.

"We'll see," she murmured.

"Marianne," he cajoled. "I really can. It would be so much better than that thing you have me bouncing around on." He smiled encouragingly at her, despite his having to cough again.

"I'm sorry if it's uncomfortable," she apologized. "It was easier than carrying you."

He laughed. "I'm sure it was." He stretched mightily. "I need to exercise. Where are we going? Do you know the way, now?"

Marianne looked at Will from sad eyes, contemplating her reply. "I'm not held back by the pull of your civilization now. We will go home."

"Is it far?"

"Not anymore, it's not. But, get a good night's sleep. Tomorrow will be long for you."

As it turned out, she was much closer to Brighton than she had figured. Late the following morning, as they topped a southern ridge, she could see what was left of the once familiar town site. "Oh, my!" She exclaimed.

Will looked at her, then down at the ruins of the town. "This is it?"

"This was Brighton," she nodded assent, her voice a whisper.

"What now?"

"Let's go down and take a look around." She looked toward the south, but the river and the hills overlooking it were obscured. "Then we'll see what else might be left."

"Marianne, if we turned around right now...."

"No!" She said emphatically, shaking her head.

He sighed. "There's no one here, Marianne."

In answer, she marched down the hill on an angle, away from him to his right. "Wait!" He yelled, but had to follow to keep her in sight. She walked resolutely down one hill, then veered to her right and went up another, crossing the ravine in between like a young deer, over and under windfalls and patches of brambles. About half way up the second hill, William had to stop. He couldn't keep up this insane pace in his weakened condition. He plopped himself down on a log and bowed his head to his knees, gasping for air. The gasping brought about wheezing and the wheezing caused him to cough.

When William finally got control of his breath, Marianne was standing before him, hands on hips. "We're not going back," she said.

He stared at her from baleful eyes while he concentrated on breathing normally. He swallowed, then swallowed again. "I can't keep up with you, let alone fight you."

"Then quit trying. There's a cabin on top of the hill," she pointed behind herself. "We can rest there."

"Does someone live there?" He asked hopefully.

"Not any more." She shook her head sadly. "They've all gone away." She held out an arm. "Can you walk up there?"

"I don't know." He said in resignation. "I think so, but not if it's very far."

"It's not."

She helped him onto his feet, steadying him next to her. He took a couple of tentative steps, then a few more. Finally, with her help, he climbed the hill to the top. A crude cabin with a sod roof met his gaze. There were a few fruit trees and one big elm for shade. It was a pastoral sight, something right out of the pages of a book. As they moved toward the cabin, he could see a corral and a small barn behind the house. The barn had partially burned, and some of the fence, but the cabin seemed to be intact. They stopped at the door. Almost reverently, Marianne called out. "Diana? Edward?" There was no answer, so she led William inside. There obviously had been an exodus from this home. No personal things, the ones that make a house a home, were left. Marianne walked through the four small rooms in a daze. "Where could they have gone? The house is still standing. Why would they move, and with her mother?" she sighed. "Of course, the village is all burned away, now."

"Perhaps they thought this house would burn and moved away, or went to help others," William offered. He slumped onto a bench along one wall of the main room. He was exhausted, and he could feel the tightness in his chest indicating that the pneumonia hadn't left him. He needed bed rest, liquids, and some penicillin. *Now, where are we going to get that?* He smiled ruefully. "Even some sulfa drugs would help, anything!" He muttered. "Marianne, what herbs have you been giving me? I need something to help me."

She looked at him as though she only now remembered he was with her. "I'm sorry, Will."

She looked around carefully. There was no bedding on the bedsteads. Marianne made many trips to the barn for straw and hay to make soft beds. She put their own bedding on a bed stead for herself and spread his and Anita's sleeping bags on the bed in the main room, the one that had been Diana's mother's bed. "There, you lie down and rest." She said, helping William onto the soft bedding. "I'll get a fire going and make you some tea. Your fever is up again." She sighed. "I need Diana to help me fight this."

She busied herself making a fire in the ancient-looking, rock fireplace, using their own camp pot for boiling water. While it was heating, she went outside to hunt for herbs. She noticed the tracks in the dirt that showed how Diana, or someone had loaded a wagon or carriage, maybe both. They drove away toward Marianne's old home. She stared away to the east for a few moments. *Would they have moved over there?* She wondered, then shook her head in answer to her own question. *The cabin is too small for three people to live comfortably. But, maybe they aren't comfortable, just safe from the fires.* She looked toward the east again, but couldn't see any telltale smoke from a chimney. Of course, the light was fast fading, so maybe she just couldn't see. With a little seed of hope in her heart, she went back inside where she prepared some tea and gave it to William. He drank it greedily, then drank some warm water as well. That was a good sign. *He wants fluids now,* she thought. *If I can find Diana, together we can make him well.*

She brought some more straw in from the barn and made up another bed in Diana's room. She spread a blanket she found on a shelf over the straw. It was remarkably comfortable. She would sleep there to be closer to William. Diana could have the other bed she made earlier. She added more straw to the base of that bed, and tucked extra straw under William, too.

Morning brought a gray, fog- filled vista. Marianne made William as comfortable as she could. During the night, he had succumbed to coughing and fevers. She bathed his brow with cool herb water and forced some tea into his mouth, making him swallow. She checked Diana's root cellar and was delighted to find it about half full. She made some broth out of dried meat for William and made herself some corn mush.

William roused himself for a little while during the day, seeming conscious of her presence and where they were when she spoke to him. Then, he fell into a deep sleep. *I hope this isn't the 'death sleep'.* She prayed. "I have to leave you for just a little while, Will." She smoothed his brow with gentle fingers. "I'll be back soon. I must try to find Diana."

Marianne hurried down the road toward her old home. When she saw it, she was almost upon the doorstep, the fog was so thick. She burst through the front door, fully expecting to see her friend sitting at her own table. But, the cabin was silent. She walked numbly through the two rooms, noting that everything she had owned was gone. The shelves were empty, the chairs were missing, even the old red dress! "Who would want that old rag?"

She walked out into the garden and lovingly visited each grave of her family. With a shiver and some shock, she found the new stone with her own name and death date. "Is Marianne dead?" She asked the silent stone. She wrapped her arms around herself as she knelt before her own grave marker. "I don't feel dead." *Where am I?* Came the age-old question. *Who are you?* Echoed the reply. Marianne shuddered at the thoughts. Tears welled up and spilled down over her cheeks. She watched, horrified, as in her mind a plane crashed into the forest, setting everything on fire. It burned out quickly, causing a smokey-misty air. Two people stumbled about, making a small fire of their own. They sat dumbly before the small flames, then slowly faded into their last sleep. Marianne pictured someone exchanging the red dress for a faded homespun one. *Was that me?* She hugged herself tighter as the memories became reality once again. But, plunged almost immediately into the dream again. She was being picked up in strong arms and carried to a waiting wagon. There was the murmur of voices. As they bumped away on a trackless trail, she watched the two bodies lying on the ground near the ashes of a long-dead fire, growing smaller and smaller. *Where am I? Who are you?* The questions burned within her mind.

Instinctively now, Marianne's hand reached up to her throat for the locket. But, it was gone. She shook off the nightmares and frightening memories. She went back into the cabin and searched, but the red dress wasn't on the shelf or anywhere else any more. She turned in a daze of thought and went out to what had been her own root cellar. It too, had food in it, although not as much as she had remembered. At least he wouldn't starve. She closed the door and secured it. Then, she turned back the way she had come. The sun wasn't penetrating the fog, yet she knew it must be well after midday. She walked back to the home where Diana had once lived. "I don't even know if I am real." She muttered. "And if I'm not real, what was the purpose of all these years, if years there were?"

She went inside Diana's house to check on her patient. He was sleeping, but she woke him to drink more broth, tea, and warm water. He did so gladly, then rolled over and was almost immediately asleep again. Marianne smiled and nodded. He would live. He had a destiny with these people, wherever they were. She left him sleeping and walked down the hill to the burned-out village. The fog was thicker in the valley, if that was possible. She moved along as though floating. It was no effort for her to walk uphill or down.

She looked at the old blacksmith's shop where

her husband, Will Armstrong had worked. It was nothing but ashes and debris. She heard the sounds of someone working on wood, tapping or hammering lightly. Slowly, she drifted toward the sound. In the obscurity of the fog, she watched as Rachel worked hard to build a shelter. Marianne smiled. Rachel was wreathed in sunlight as she worked to make a place for herself. Marianne studied the girl she loved so deeply. She didn't see the deformities and infirmities. She only saw the girl she loved beyond all else. This was the driving force that brought her to this valley, the hopes and prayers of this determined wraith of a girl.

When darkness gathered around the village ruins, and Rachel retired to her bed in the root cellar, Marianne stepped up to the site and corrected some of the building, finishing one wall and restarting another so it would fit more snugly. Quietly, she moved inside and stood looking down at the girl in her sleep. *Rest well, My Girl,* she thought as she laid a hand lightly on Rachel's hair. *I'm nearby and will help you with what I can. I'll bring Diana home for you. Somehow, it will all be alright, I promise.* She shuddered as a chill passed over her. *Then, Darling, you must let me go. I understand now, and you must let me go.* She bent down and kissed the beautiful, sleeping form before walking out into the night. The fog settled around her as she picked her way up the hill where Diana's house loomed up in the fog suddenly, in front of her. Marianne turned around as she reached the small porch, peering into the fog. *The fog.* She contemplated for a moment, then nodded in understanding. *The mist, and the fog......*

Four

Into the Sun

Frederick Wilder and George Bays led out on horseback behind Thomas Woodslee. Behind them all, rolled wagons, carriages, and carts loaded with the precious goods of families on the move. They reluctantly left their temporary camp behind, but looked forward as well to a new beginning.

There had been a general conference the evening before the actual move. Many expressed anxiety about being so near what they now considered a haunted village. They viewed the young Thomas almost as a savior, come to rescue them not only from the fires, but also from years of tyranny and fears, both new and old. All the people in the little caravan had lived their entire lives in the old village, under the vengeful thumb of Sarah Stuart. Now, they felt free for the first time in many years and yet somehow apprehensive that Sarah would still have some hold over them if they tried to rebuild their lost village, or if they built a new one so close-by. Their fears were reinforced by sightings of the mysterious ghost, some of the boys had been frightened by. The stories concerning a black-shrouded girl/woman who seemed to fly or glide over the ground leaving no footprints and making no sounds became bigger and bigger. In only a few days, the sightings went from two to ten, then fifteen.

"It's the ghost of the evil one, or someone who wants to avenge her." One of the father's proclaimed.

Father Jonathan tried for awhile to explain that there were tracks of someone, that this wasn't as mysterious as they were making it, but to no avail. The people were ready to believe the worst. Perhaps they needed these stories to justify moving away from their old lives. Whatever the reason, they wouldn't listen to logic or facts. They were determined the sightings were not human, but some evil of the netherworld.

After the general community meeting concluded, Frederick, George, and Thomas lingered around the small fire near the monk's house. "What of this mystery?" Asked Thomas. "Surely, Frederick, you don't believe in ghosts, or witches, or vengeful spirits."

Frederick removed his hat and slapped it against his leg to rid it of imaginary dust. "I don't know what to believe," he mumbled. "Ever since the fires began a few years ago, we have had mysterious things happening. I don't want to think this could be someone's idea of vengeance, but I don't know what else to think. Sarah Stuart, or the evil one, as some of the villagers are calling her, held our village in total fear. We believe she killed members of her own family, and maybe even a few others. Someone finally killed her on or about the day the fires burned the village. That must mean someone is still alive and out there, somewhere." He indicated the general direction of the village.

"And it's a girl or a woman?" Thomas was filled with curiosity at their story.

"We don't know." Frederick looked at his friend, George Bays, who nodded. "We never saw her or it ourselves, only a couple of boys claimed to have seen something. All we saw was a black cat, and that for only a moment."

"Does it have to do with Will Armstrong's wife? That seemed like a mystery to me."

"I don't think so. I saw tracks up on the mountains heading outside. I think she went back where she came from." Frederick paused. "Wherever that is."

"Weren't you there when Will rescued her, then?"

Again Frederick looked at George. "We were," George answered. "We've never spoken of it since that day in the fog up there on those northwestern ridges."

"I saw the place." Thomas answered. "Will told me of it and I went up there. I've seen many wonders and know of the world beyond the Forbidden Hills. Will and I spoke of these things quite a few times."

"Did he speak of his wife, then? I mean, did he

speak of how we acquired her?" George frowned at the memory.

"Somewhat." Thomas assented. "We spoke of that and of another tale I know about. I don't believe he shared that with anyone."

"Maybe you should share that with us now." Frederick crossed his arms and looked sternly at the young man.

"I know I want to hear it," Diana stepped from the shadows where she'd been listening, and walked boldly into the firelight.

Thomas smiled at her. "I'm not surprised," he stated.

Diana settled herself on a stump to listen. "Marianne was my friend." She said.

Thomas looked up sharply. "Marianne? You called her Marianne?" He looked from one to another of them. "Will's wife?"

They were all staring at him. "Yes-s-s," said Diana cautiously.

"Is there something wrong with the name?" Frederick asked.

"No. No, not at all." He shook his head, a thoughtful look upon his brow. "All in good time. One of you, please tell your story, then I'll tell you mine. It's time, I think."

Frederick and George gazed at one another for a few seconds. Then, Frederick exhaled long and began to speak. "We traveled up to the fires after hearing the roar and explosion. We found the site. You say you've been there, so you know what we saw."

"I don't." Diana asserted.

George Bays explained. "There are things beyond the Forbidden Hills that we just don't speak of because no one would believe us. This was one of those things."

"Do you mean one of the great flying machines of the outside world?" She asked.

The men were stunned. They didn't know Will Armstrong had confided these things to Diana.

"Yes," George nodded in answer.

"Thank you."

Frederick scratched his head and shook it before continuing. "No one was alive at the site. A couple of people had tried to survive, but they were close to death when we arrived. There was a man and a woman. The woman had red hair." Frederick closed his eyes as the memories flooded his mind. "Will was mesmerized by her. He tried to revive her, but it did no good. He sat a long time looking at her, his hands in her hair."

"We finally asked him if he wanted us to bury the two survivors," George picked up the story.

"He told us no, but that seemed to finally break through whatever thoughts he was having and suddenly he was in a hurry to get the wagon down off the mountain. We were more than glad to oblige. We put out what fires there were, and started down the old trail."

"She wasn't from the wreckage?" Diana asked in amazement.

"No, er, let me finish." Frederick answered.

"Excuse me, I just always assumed that part."

"Yes, well, we'd gone about a mile or two down the trail when we heard a cry, like an animal or something in pain."

Diana's head came up with renewed interest at the similarity to her own experience after leaving the village just days before.

"Will stopped the horses and turned back. We couldn't see anything. He jumped down, walking along the trail. We just looked at each other for a few minutes. Finally, Will was yelling at us to come and help him. We ran to him, but what we saw made us stop dead in our tracks." He shifted on his seat and wiped at his sweating forehead. "There on the roadway was that girl from the site. Will was bent over her, trying to talk to her." He stopped and mopped at his perspiring brow.

George began. "I didn't know what to think." He said. "I looked at Frederick and he looked at me. Will was giving orders to help him carry her to the wagon. She had two crude kind of canes with her. I carried one and he carried the other." He indicated Frederick. "Will just picked her up and carried her, with us trailing behind them."

"Then she was alive when you left the site!" Diana exclaimed. "How on earth did she ever catch up to you?"

"That's what I asked." Frederick answered.

"I wondered about her dress," George said quietly. "At the site I thought she had on an old homespun dress. But, now she had on that red one you saw her in when we got down to the village." He spoke directly to Diana.

"What are you saying? She changed clothes before she came after you?" Diana was incredulous. "She couldn't have done that, she was much too badly injured!"

"I know. She was burned bad and had broken bones." George shook his head. "The girl I looked at up there by the fire, was dead already, I'm sure of it. So was the man. He didn't show up anywhere, just this Marianne."

"We don't know how it happened." Frederick explained. "But, it did."

"And yet," mused George. "There was something..." He shook his head, bewildered still at the feelings from so long ago.

They both became quiet. Diana was looking at them in shock. Thomas seemed amused. "I wondered how it happened." He said thoughtfully. "Now, let me tell you my story."

"Please do," begged Diana. "I'm having trouble with theirs." She waved a hand at the other two men.

"Let's see, it must have been twelve or fourteen seasons ago, I think," he began. "My father and I were on one of our trips to find ore. We'd been over to talk to Will Armstrong. He'd told me about some of the deaths and tragedies in your village around that time. I think it was when your mill burned down."

They all acknowledged his statement.

"On our way home, we came across a woman laying half in the creek, not far from our village. I thought she was dead, but Father stopped to take the body to the village for burial. We'd never seen her before. She was young, late teens or early twenties, with black hair and lots of freckles."

"That sounds like Ruth," Diana murmured.

"It couldn't be Ruth." Frederick said. "She died right here. I know we buried her."

"I know," she said. "I was just commenting."

Thomas was tolerant of their discussion, then he resumed the telling. "My father, like Will after him, carried the woman to our village where our healers," he smiled and nodded at Diana, "cured her of her injuries. She had been burned and had some broken ribs, I believe. She hovered between life and death for many weeks, but finally was able to get around, but she was never to remember who she was or where she had come from. She managed to have a happy life despite it all. She taught our children songs, and rhymes, and stories. She sewed for the community and took part in our varied activities. There were times over the years, as I grew, that I saw her up on the ridges, looking down on the village, or in the fields, staring up into the heavens. When

I asked her what she saw, she smiled at me and said her destiny called her. I never understood what it was she was talking about. I was very young and she was a mysterious, older woman." He smiled at the memory. "A few years ago, maybe three or four, she disappeared. We searched for a day or two, but to no avail. When I heard about Will's wife, I wondered if it was our own Mary, for that is what we named her. But, I understand Will's wife had red hair and her eyes were green. We never thought of it again, although we have always wondered what became of Mary." He grew silent.

The silence spread to them all as they sat before the fire and contemplated the story. Finally, Diana broke the quiet. "If we are to believe this," she began. "I mean, I'm sure you're telling us the truth, but it's so incredible." She faltered. "What I mean is, if these two stories are true then Marianne, or Mary, whoever she is, doesn't exist as we know life to be."

"But she was real!" George exclaimed.

"Yes, she was," Thomas said quietly. "She was as real as you and me." He pointed at them all and himself last. "At least, our Mary was real."

"Marianne was certainly real," Diana recalled. "I administered to her myself. I helped her birth her children." She looked at Thomas. "What do you make of this?"

"I don't know what to tell you," he answered. "The implications are completely beyond my reckoning." They lapsed into another short silence. "One thing I find interesting though," he paused, contemplating. "When I found her, there was a deep fog upon the mountain. If I remember your own story correctly, you were shrouded in the same deep, misty fog."

"True," asserted Frederick. "There was smoke and fog and an overlying mist that made us all shiver with the dampness, and visibility was almost nothing. We had to lead the horses on the steepest parts of the trail."

"Where did she come from?" Diana voiced the thought for them all.

"Are we to assume, then, that Mary and Marianne are one and the same person?" George asked in shock.

"I don't know," Thomas shook his head with the wonder of their tales. "How many women could there be wandering around out there in the foggy mountains?"

"And now she's just walked away into someone else's life?" Diana asked no one in particular.

"What was the purpose in her coming here at all?" George asked.

"I've wondered that same thing," Frederick added.

"Well, she certainly added purpose to Will Armstong's life," Diana said. "He loved her deeply." A tear escaped down her cheek. She wiped it away with the hem of her skirt.

"They had those children, but not one of them lived." Commented George. "I wonder if things would have been different for them if the children had lived."

"Rachel always thought Marianne was her mother." Diana mused. "Now, I wonder the same thing."

"I helped Elias Stuart bury his son and Ruth, his daughter-in-law. It can't be her." Frederick asserted.

"Who's Rachel?" Thomas asked. "I don't recall any Rachel among your group."

"Poor Rachel," Diana said sadly. "She died, too. Probably at the same hand that killed her own parents."

"How did this person get so much power over the whole village? She killed, yet never came to be judged or punished, it seems."

"Nothing could ever really be proved against her," Frederick explained. "She was a sly, old She-Devil."

"I'm afraid that's true." They all looked around at the voice from the shadows. Father Jonathan stepped out to greet them. "I wondered what all the chatting was about. I should have known."

"Did you hear Thomas' tale, Father?" George asked the old monk.

"No," he shook his head. "I just heard the comments about Rachel and Sarah."

"Thomas, tell him your story," Frederick commanded quietly.

So, the tale was told again for the benefit of their spiritual leader. As Thomas related his story, Diana offered commentary. It didn't take long to tell.

"Then, Marianne didn't come from the outside world? She has been living among the villages for nearly fifteen years?"

"It would seem so," Thomas nodded.

"I always knew there was something wrong, or if not wrong at least something more we weren't getting to, but I didn't know what it was." He spoke more to himself than to the company. "Did Brother Armstrong know, do you think?" He asked.

"Know what, Father? What is it you think we know?" Frederick asked.

"Well, I mean, do you think he knew Marianne was some kind of changeling or chameleon creature?"

"Oh, Father!" Diana said in dismay. "What a thing to say!"

"Mary, as we called our mysterious woman," explained Thomas. "Was human. She wasn't some mythical character. I cannot explain her presence, nor can you, it seems, explain the presence of Marianne. None the less, they were real enough."

"But, then what are we to think? How will this be explained to the community?"

"Why does it ever need to go any farther than this?" Thomas asked. "She's gone again. We are likely to never see her. Perhaps some other village is in need of her. She was always talking of her destiny, whatever that meant."

"I wonder," said Diana.

"What is it you wonder, Child?" Father Jonathan asked.

"No." Diana shook her head. "It sounds foolish even as I form the idea."

"Let us judge," Thomas said kindly.

"The boys saw someone, once in the village and then at the wood lot. If this person can take on other identities, could she appear to them like a witch?"

"Why should she do that?" Thomas asked. "Both times she appeared, if it is the same person at all, she was a kindly woman, full of love and charity."

"That's true."

"Then why turn evil now? What would there be to gain by doing that? Why suddenly scare everyone, especially the children?" He shook his head. "No, the children were especially fond of Mary."

"Hmmmmm," responded Diana. You know, we don't know the apparition was evil, just different and somehow frightening to some young boys. Maybe she wasn't even trying to frighten them." She paused. "Perhaps it wasn't even Mary or Marianne."

"Why, though?" George persisted.

"To get us to all go away. Maybe she wants to be alone, after all. Perhaps," Diana stumbled for words again. "Perhaps her destiny was to be with Will, if it were Marianne, and now she is lost..." Her voice trailed off. "I don't know. It's all crazy!"

Frederick interrupted. "I saw with my own eyes that she, Marianne, left the area for the outside world. I know it was her tracks I saw. And, come to think of it, I don't believe ghosts or apparitions leave solid tracks. What of that?"

"Perhaps she wanted to leave those signs." Diana offered.

"Again, why?" George asked.

"You know," Diana was thinking deeply. "When Uncle Edward and I came back from the house, we came through the village. I told Father Jonathan what we saw there, a little shack built out by the Stuart's root cellar. Perhaps she's built that instead of the boys. We thought maybe they were just playing tricks on the adults so they could play at the old village alone. Maybe it is Marianne."

"Why would she build a little shack, as you call it? She could just go to her old house." George stated.

"Or to yours, Diana, it's still standing," Thomas added.

"I don't know." Diana hung her head and rubbed her hands over her hair. "Why has any of this happened? Maybe the memories of her dead family are too much for her up at the old cabin. I just don't know!"

"It's a good thing we are leaving in the morning," Father Jonathan said. "It is time to leave all the mystery and fear behind us. Perhaps that is why she came, to rid us of the fear."

"Do you think she killed Sarah?" Diana asked.

"Someone did," said Frederick.

The talking was over. There was no more that could be said and no differences or help to be had.

The group slowly dispersed. Diana walked in deep thought, back to the tent she was now sharing with her uncle. He was snoring loudly, so she didn't disturb him with the news she had heard. It would keep.

Now, on this bright morning, they were in the line, moving slowly away from all Diana ever knew. They climbed up a winding path into a green and healthy forest. The scent of the pines was overwhelming, comforting their minds and healing their hearts. The second and third days were much the same, plodding along through the deep forest, following a winding trail. They spent the nights in small clearings or meadows where streams meandered through. The fourth night on the trail, they camped in a clearing high on a mountain bluff. They could see the winding, silvery ribbon of the river and the blackened forest they were leaving behind. "Is that smoke?" Diana asked Thomas as they looked at the vista spread before them.

"Where?"

"Off there, to the northwest?"

He shielded his eyes against the setting sun. "Perhaps, but only a small tendril of it, a
single fire or campfire, I would say."

Diana grasped his arm. "I'm going back," she said. "Someone's still there, and I mean to know who it is."

"Don't go alone," he advised.

"Then who should I take with me?"

"I'll go." He answered. "Just let me get these

people settled in the valley and I'll go with you."

"It can't wait, Thomas," she said. "Something tells me it cannot wait for a week or two. I must go now."

"Let's bring it up to Frederick," he said. "He'll know what to do."

"No!" Father Jonathan exploded when they approached him, in company with Frederick and George. "No one is ever going back there!"

"Father," cajoled George Bays. "Frederick and I have walked over these mountains all our lives. We'll take Diana back to see what we can see."

"A woman!" Father Jonathan admonished. "A single woman with two men."

"She's a healer, Father," Uncle Edward said softly. "If there is something wrong, she, more than anyone else, will be of help. I think the lass is right. She should go." He paused. "She can't go alone." He splayed his hands in supplication.

"He's right," Frederick put in. "We'll go back tomorrow on horseback. It will be quicker. The rest of you can go ahead and get us all settled. We'll be back to help in a matter of a few days, I'm sure." He paused, looking back toward the old village. "Diana's right. There is smoke out there. Someone is left behind."

"Be careful, my Dear Girl," Uncle Edward said to his niece. "I know what it is that drives you, but be careful."

She stared long into his kind eyes. "I will, I

promise. Thank you for your undying faith in me."

"I don't like it," said Father Jonathan. He put up a hand to ward off any more argument. "Go with my blessing, but don't expect me to like it."

In the morning, the company split. The bulk of them climbed the last hill before descending into the new valley. Thomas had been right. The people there greeted them all with open arms. They had already designated the southmost end of their lush valley to the newcomers. There, they had begun a few log houses, and were clearing more spots for others. The new group would be about a mile from the main community, on their own, yet close enough to be neighborly and take part in community activities. There was much to do, digging wells, building barns and fences, dividing up the parcels of land they had inherited from the generous folks of Thomas' city. For such they deemed the larger community because it was so much larger than their old village of Brighton. In a happy celebration they christened their tiny village New Brighton. The burned out forest and the fog seemed all left behind them.

Five

Forgetting and Remembering

Three riders went back toward the devastation of the fires. They rode in silence broken only by the clopping of their horses hooves on the stony path, and the creak of leather from their saddles. Diana was weary by the time they got to their night's camp. The short breaks they'd taken during the day hadn't been restful. She was anxious to get back to the old village and the men with her seemed to be also, so they pressed on until the horses couldn't go another step. After a hasty meal, Diana rolled up in a blanket with her head against her saddle and went directly into an exhausted sleep.

They were up once again with the first pale light of dawn. As they rode down into the valley of soot and ashes, fog rose up to meet them. Frederick called a halt and they sat on their horses while he sniffed the air for any sign of smoke. "No, it's fog," he said finally. "There's no fresh smoke smell. Let's be careful, now." They rode on, coming at last to the wood lot, then to the edge of the old village.

"I smell smoke now," Diana offered.

They stopped again. "It's a stove or campfire, not the forest," observed George who was riding behind her. "It's just a whiff of smoke on the air, then gone again. That means a cooking or camp fire."

Frederick was riding off to the left and couldn't get a whiff of what they were smelling. They walked their horses slowly down the main street of the old village. There wasn't much to see even if the skies had been clear. The village was destroyed. "Show us that shack you saw," said George.

Diana rode ahead of them, but the fog was so thick they were to the creek at the end of the village before they knew it. "We've passed it," Diana said. "It's at Sarah's old place."

They turned their horses around and rode back a few hundred feet, then dismounted and walked. Suddenly they could see the jumbled mass of the old Stuart barn to their left. "There!" Diana exclaimed. "It's only a few feet from the old barn, a shack built onto the root cellar."

They peered into the fog, walking very slowly. At last they could make out the shape of the little board room added to the root cellar. "It's not half bad for children's work," Frederick said as he ran a hand over the structure. He tried to open the door, but it was fastened from the inside. There were windows, but they too, were shuttered and barred from inside the building.

George tapped on the water barrel. "This is full,"

he commented. "They've put in a lot of work here." He scratched his head. "This doesn't seem to be the work of playing children. This is a shelter, not a play fort. When would they have had time to do this much work?"

"I've been wondering that, too," said Frederick. "Maybe Diana's idea is more to the mark."

Diana had walked to the back of the cellar and found the covered entrance there. It opened easily for her. She shut it again and walked around to the front where the men were discussing what to do next. "I've found a way in," she said in a quiet tone. "There's a tunnel at the back."

They walked to the back of the cellar where Diana showed them the small tunnel. Frederick hunkered down to look inside. "It must be the boys," he said. "I couldn't get through there."

"I might be able to wriggle in there," Diana said. "Then I could open the door for you men."

"You don't know what you'll find in there," observed George. He looked furtively at the trees behind them. "I keep feeling like someone's watching us."

They were still speaking softly, just above a whisper. "Yes," Diana said. "I've felt it too." She looked back at the forest as well, scanning the nearby trees.

"I think the place is empty," said Frederick. "Go ahead in there if you can, Sister Macklin. It will be easy enough to break down that front door if we hear anything wrong."

Diana lowered herself to the ground, then crawled and wriggled head first into the hole. She soon came against another door at the end of the tunnel. It too, pushed open easily. She crawled out inside the root cellar. It was dark and musty smelling, the smell of earth. Diana stood for a few moments until her eyes adjusted to the meager light from the tunnel. She slowly walked up the few steps to the little room. There was muted light from a few cracks in the boards of the walls. She walked to the door and took down the bar holding it shut. It opened easily on its leather hinges, hanging a little askew. The men stepped into the little room, bending over to keep from hitting their heads on the ceiling. The room was dwarfed even more by their presence. "There's no one here," she said.

"Someone's been living here, though," said Frederick.

"Yes," Diana agreed as she walked around looking at the dishes and furnishings. She recognized it all. "These are Marianne's things," she breathed. She looked at George and Frederick who stood awkwardly in the middle of the room. "Her house didn't burn, why would she move everything down here?"

"Well, we know now this isn't the work of children." George said. "Someone is living here." He lifted the lid on the small stove and closed it again. "The stove has warm ashes in it."

"That wasn't the smoke we smelled then,"

Frederick said.

"No, it wasn't."

"Could someone else be living up on the hill?" Asked Diana. "The smoke would come down into the valley in this dampness. "Or maybe whoever was here moved up there."

"Everyone is accounted for, except maybe, Marianne," said Frederick. "If she came back, why would she have two places? Why would she have a fire overnight in this crude cabin, then build a new fire up at, say, your place, Sister Macklin?"

"I don't know. Maybe she built this before she found her own house was still standing and now she's gone up there." Diana shrugged.

"Then why is her stuff still here? And why would there be coals in the stove, yet smoke from up the hill?"

"I don't think the smoke smell can be from the Armstrong cabin, you know," interjected George. "It would go down the river, I think. Why would she be at your cabin?" The men both looked askance at Diana.

"I don't know!" Diana was frustrated with these men looking at her for all the answers. They weren't really, but she felt the burden because it had been her idea to come back to the village. "Let's close this back up like we found it," she said quietly. "I feel like we've violated someone's privacy." The men agreed and soon she found herself crawling out the hole in the back of the root cellar. She stood and closed the little door, draping the leather apron back over it as she had found it in the beginning. She took one last look at the blackened forest, then turned to walk away.

"Diana...," came the whisper from the trees.

"What?" She whirled toward the forest, looking wildly for the speaker. "Who is it? Marianne, is it you?" She looked frantically, walking back toward the burned trees. She heard a whimper and the scurrying of some animal or person running lightly. "Come back!" She called.

"What is it?" Frederick called as he and George joined her. "What's wrong?"

"Someone spoke my name," she said now. The sound of her voice echoed in the trees. "I heard someone or something moving over there, toward the barn." She pointed to her left.

Frederick went to look in the ruins of the barn. George stayed with Diana. "Are you sure of what you heard?" He asked. "Could it have been an animal or the wind?"

Diana held very still. The trees were swaying gently in a light breeze. She could feel it on her cheek. The fog was lifting, too. She shook her head. "I'm sure I heard my name, then a kind of cry or moan. Maybe someone is hurt."

Frederick rejoined them. "Nothing in the barn. Someone's been working in there, most likely when they built this little place here," he indicated the room on the root cellar. "Looks like they hauled water up from the creek to fill the barrel. Someone is planning to stay here quite a while."

"That stove in there is one Will Armstrong built for us long ago," George observed.

"Whoever it is, built them a sled to haul heavy things on. He's smart."

"He?" Diana asked.

"Well, we don't know who it is, do we?" Frederick answered.

"I'm betting on Marianne," she answered. "A woman could have done this." She looked appreciatively at the room.

The men looked skeptical, but wisely said not another word about it.

Suddenly, George lifted his head and sniffed the air. "Smell that smoke?" He asked.

"Yes," Frederick answered.

Diana nodded. "It's coming from up the hill. Someone is cooking up at my place."

"I think you're right," Frederick said. "It's too close to be out at Will's place."

Without another word, they walked to their horses and mounted to ride up to Diana's old cabin. Diana looked back at the barn and blackened stumps of trees. "I'll be back!" She called, then said more quietly. "I'll be back." There was no answer, but she didn't really expect one. She turned her horse to follow the men up the hill.

The fog grew thicker, the higher they went. "It isn't normal for the fog to be thicker up here than in the valley," Frederick said. "We should be breaking out into sunshine." But, they didn't. The horses plodded along, heads down in the heavy, wet clouds. The smell of smoke was heavier, too and for a few moments they worried about the cabin burning. But, abruptly, it seemed, the cabin loomed before them, first as a black, nondescript box, then as the cabin, itself. The door was open and they could hear the sound of coughing. "I'll go first," Frederick said.

"That sounds like a man," Diana offered lamely as she dismounted. She held the horses for them all as the men approached the cabin. Without taking her eyes off the men for more than a moment, she tied the horses to the railing near the corral, then moved cautiously toward the cabin, her bag of herbs held tightly in her hand. It wasn't long before they came scrambling back out of the cabin and to her. They both looked very frightened.

"It's...it's...," stuttered George. Frederick walked to the fence without saying anything, just staring out into the fog.

"It's what?" Diana asked urgently. "What's wrong?"

The two men looked long at each other, past Diana as though she wasn't even there. Then Frederick spoke. "Go look for yourself," he wiped at the dampness on his face. "I, it can't be what we thought."

Diana looked toward the cabin, then back at her companions. Sunlight suddenly appeared, burning off the fog and warming the air quickly. The cabin was bathed in its light. Diana looked up at the fast-spreading blue of the sky. "It's a sign," she said quietly. "Everything will be fine." She turned abruptly, leaving them both standing by the corrals.

Diana approached the cabin carefully. She gathered her damp skirt as she stepped over the threshold into her old home. On her mother's platform lay a man. Diana stopped, peering closer. "No!" She breathed. "It can't be!" She walked closer and laid a cool hand on his fevered brow. "Will, is that you?" She asked. Even as she said it aloud, she knew it wasn't true. The man closely resembled Will Armstrong, but it wasn't him. This man was younger, more her own age. He was slighter of build, although muscular. He was wracked with chills and fever and the healer inherent within her took over. She immediately went to work, making healing tea and a warm wash. Water was already boiling at the fireplace, so she could proceed quickly. It was a good thing, for this man was very ill. She wasn't sure he would live through the next few hours. There was meat and some flat bread in the oven on the side of her fireplace. She knew it couldn't have been this man cooking a meal like that. And the cabin was cleaned. Someone else had been here with him. As she put a meal on the table for herself and the two men with her, she mumbled. "Are you here somewhere, Marianne? Is this your doing?" She looked around the room, but there was no answer. She went to the door and called softly to the two men at the corrals. They had busied themselves caring for the horses.

Frederick, George, and Diana ate the meal and prepared to spend the night at the cabin. There was plenty of fresh straw and bedding on the two bedsteads used by herself and her uncle when they lived in the cabin. Frederick assured her there was no one else nearby. He'd checked around the barn and corrals, even turned the horses loose into the field to graze, and saw no one.

"Well, someone put straw down on the bedsteads, swept out the cabin, and fixed this food," Diana observed. "And it wasn't him." She quietly pointed to the man on the bed. His breathing was labored. Diana went to him with a bowl of broth. It was all she and Frederick could do to get a little liquid down his throat.

"It isn't Brother Armstrong, is it?" Frederick looked searchingly at Diana.

"No," she shook her head. "He's not our Will."

"Well, he looks enough like him to scare me," George offered from his place by the door.

"I think we're all looking for ghosts," Diana said softly.

They smiled knowingly at one another, then said their good nights. "I'll take first watch," Diana said. "In case he worsens." The men went to sleep in Uncle Edward's and Diana's beds. Diana sat comfortably at the foot of her mother's bed, close to her patient.

Sometime during the night, the man awoke. His fever had broken and he was drenched with his own sweat. He looked out of fever sore eyes at Diana, thrashing wildly on the bed. "Anita?" He asked, reaching toward Diana. "Did you bring help?" His voice was weak and raspy. Then he fell back into the blankets and a dark delirium. He called alternately for Anita and Marianne.

Diana smiled at his fevered talk. *He knows Marianne,* she thought. Now she was certain Marianne had come back and was living in the valley. *She's taking care of this man as best she can up here, and must be living in the little shack she built down in the valley.* But, that didn't make sense. *Why doesn't she just stay up here with him? He needs almost constant care right now.* Diana prayed for the man to live so he could explain some of the mystery to them. She looked fondly at him as she bathed his face and arms. *He looks so much like Will,* she thought. Memories flooded her mind as she thought of all the years she spent loving Will Armstrong from afar, sure she would someday marry the handsome village blacksmith. They spent time together doing good things for the village people, sharing hopes and dreams. She believed Will thought they would marry some day as well. "But then Marianne had come to them, and she had married Will. *Then he died, and a little of me died, too.* Diana sighed at the thought. It was a mournful sound in the room where all the men were sleeping. *Is that why she brought you back here, because you remind her of Will?* Diana looked again at her patient, then rose and checked on his breathing and temperature. He was cooler and his breathing was easier. She nodded her head in satisfaction. He was going to heal, she was sure. Her hand lingered on his cheek, one finger tracing the outline of his jaw to the point of his chin. *You do look like Will, but I think you're even more handsome.* She blushed at the thought and hastily straightened the covers. She turned the lamp down and went to her own bed of straw on her old bedstead. George rose to watch over the patient. "He's better," she whispered. "He's sleeping now." She was asleep herself almost before her head was laying on the straw pillow.

So it went for four days and nights with only slight improvement in her patient. The men hunted and roamed the area in search of anything that might help them in their new life. On the fourth day, they were forced to remain near the cabin. The fog and mist was so thick they couldn't go out except to feed the horses. The man on the bed seemed a little more alert. He ate what was put before him and tried to sit up. His cough was nearly gone, but he still had a lingering fever.

Finally, in the pale light of yet another fog shrouded morning, Diana awoke to the low rumble of male voices. She could smell the aroma of mush and meat from the cooking fire. She stirred, but did not rise. It was delicious to wake up in her own house again, and she lay in her bed savoring the moment. The cabin door shut and the noise of voices ceased. Diana sat up and ran a hand over her tangled hair. She smoothed out her dress as best she could, picking off lingering pieces of straw. She went out the back door to the wash stand where she splashed water onto her face and arms and wet down her hair before combing it out and pulling it back into a long braid. She then went into the kitchen and got herself a bowl of food. She glanced at the bed where her patient was supposed to be. *Where is he?* She thought with a little panic. *Surely he didn't die in the night and George and Frederick are out burying him!* She rushed to the door and stepped onto the porch. Out by the corrals stood three men, talking quietly as they leaned on the rails of the fence. She watched as George quickly went into the barn and came out with a keg he put behind the stranger and both Frederick and George helped him to sit. Frederick squatted to be closer to the stranger while George leaned against a fencepost. They both seemed mesmerized by the stranger's conversation. A picture flashed into her mind of Will Armstrong sitting with these same men, discussing affairs of the village and the adventures they all shared from trips into the forested mountains. A sudden peace and contentment filled her as she watched. She smiled into the gloomy morning, then went back inside where she busied herself with her own breakfast and cleaning up their meal. She took the bedding from the bedsteads and hung them on the porch railing to air out. They would be fresh for her patient when he was ready to go back to sleep. As she turned to reenter the cabin, a movement away from the cabin caught her eye. She stepped down from the porch and walked a few feet from the cabin trying to see better. The sun was starting to burn off the fog and she could feel its warmth on her back as she walked toward the receding line of clouds. There it was again, off to her left! She ran forward a few paces. She could see a figure standing inside the fog line. It seemed to move with the fog as it was wafting away from her. "Who are you?" She cried. "Marianne? Is it you?" The figure seemed to grow completely still as the fog moved around its form. Diana ventured a few steps closer. She could hear someone running up behind her and knew the men had heard her cry. She put a hand out behind her to stop whoever it was from spoiling the moment. "Marianne," she said in a pleading tone. Marianne looked at her then, for it was indeed she. She smiled, then disappeared as quickly as the dissipating fog surrounding her. Diana stood still as she watched the sunlight spread over the hill and into the burned forest beyond.

"It was her," whispered George Bays from behind Diana.

"I know," nodded Diana. She turned to smile at him and took his arm as they walked back to the two men by the corral.

"It was her," George said as they approached the corral. Frederick nodded.

"She disappeared with the fog, right?" Asked the man sitting on the keg. His voice was deep and resonant, just as Will Armstrong's had been, but with a curious accent.

Diana smiled again. "Diana Macklin," she offered her hand to the man.

"William Avery," he answered, shaking her hand weakly. "Forgive me if I don't get up," he leaned back heavily on the fence post.

"William?" She asked in astonishment.

"Yes," he smiled tolerantly. "I understand a relative of mine might have lived here."

Diana stared at him. "A relative?" She asked breathlessly.

"I'm sorry," he apologized. "I was teasing you. Perhaps a better explanation is that someone who looked like me and shared my Christian name, lived here before me."

Diana still stared. She couldn't begin to explain what she was feeling and she knew if she tried to speak she would make a complete fool of herself. She couldn't think, she could only stare, then she began to wonder if she wasn't making a fool of herself anyway. She nodded weakly.

William, himself, broke the awkward silence. Pointing toward the porch, he asked quietly of no one in particular. "How soon could I go back to my bed?"

Diana looked at the porch, then back at William. "Oh, of course!" She exclaimed. "I was airing your bedding. It hasn't been out very long, but perhaps long enough to have freshened a little." She began walking to the porch. "We don't have extras here, now." She finished lamely. George scurried after her to help while Frederick brought William back to the cabin.

"Thank you, thank you all." William closed his eyes as he lay back against the bedding. He was asleep almost instantly, his breathing even although Diana could still detect a rattle from his lungs. She brought him a small cup of herb tea from the hearth.

"William," she said softly as she lifted his head. "Drink just a little more of this." She held the cup to his lips and he drank it all.

"Will it make me well?" He whispered.

"It is what's making you well." She answered. "This brew and your willingness to live." He smiled as he drifted back into healing sleep.

During the time of healing, Frederick and George explored the little shack in the village. "Someone is living in it," Frederick reported to Diana and William on the second evening. "But, whoever it is hides whenever we come near. There's no way to approach it unseen. We even tried to sneak up on her by night, but the slightest sound sends her scurrying out the back and into the forest. Then, she won't come back for hours. By daylight, it's no use."

"You keep saying 'she'," remarked Diana. "Is it Marianne, then?"

The two men looked thoughtfully at one another. "No," Frederick finally answered. "This girl or woman doesn't hide in the fog. She's real enough. But, it's not Marianne."

"She looks more like a small version of Sarah

Stuart," offered George. "She wears that black cloak over her dress."

Diana frowned. "All of our people are gone," she mused. "Who..." she trailed off in thought.

One evening, while the men ate their supper, Diana sat on the porch with William. The night was clear and calm, a little of the day's warmth still filled the air. "This is a beautiful spot," William said.

"Yes, it is lovely. We spent many good days here." She answered, looking out over the moonlit hills. "On a still night like this, we could see the smoke from Marianne's chimney."

"I'd like to see where she lived." He commented.

"Why?"

"I don't know. I thought that's where she was leading me, but we stopped here and I understand this is your home."

She turned to look at his shadowy form near the door of the cabin. "It is, or was." She paused, looking back over the silvery landscape, then turned her gaze to her guest once again. "Are you going to leave us soon?"

He smiled at her even though he knew she couldn't see him. "I don't think that's possible, Diana." When there was no response from her, he added. "The fog is gone."

"Yes," she answered simply. "Do you remember where you came from?" She asked after another short pause.

"Yes, I do, perfectly." He answered. "Fred and George asked me the same thing."

"Really, Will? Do you really remember? Marianne never could recall a thing." She blushed then, at having been so familiar with him. "Forgive me, Brother Avery. I forgot myself. I shouldn't have used your name so lightly."

He laughed easily. "I'm not used to formality, Diana. Should I be calling you Sister?"

"That's our way," she offered. Silence filled the night for a few moments.

"I remember everything." He said again. "I understand Marianne had amnesia when she was with you. But, I'm not that fortunate. I can remember everything from my childhood to today." He paused to cough. "I had a wonderful childhood, you know." He reminisced. "I played baseball all through school, then I went to college to become a veterinarian."

"A what?"

"A vet..." he laughed. The sound of it filled her heart with a longing to hear more. Will Armstrong never laughed aloud that she recalled. "An animal doctor," he explained.

"In your world, you had doctors just for animals?" She asked with awe.

"Yes," he laughed again.

"So you are a doctor for what kind of animals?" She asked with interest.

"I never became a vet, uh, an animal doctor. I became a surgeon of people."

"A surgeon?"

"Yes, a doctor for people." He smiled again. "Like you."

"You're a physician, like in the scriptures?" She asked. "You can heal and you know medicines and how to fix broken bones, things like that?"

He was a little taken aback. "I guess I am a physician," he answered.

"Oh," she answered. "Then my healer's art must seem very primitive to you."

"I find it intriguing. I know nothing of the healing herbs. I would like to learn, if you would want to teach me."

She thought for a long time, not speaking, but enjoying the quiet companionship she was feeling. "It would take a lifetime to teach you such things," she broke into the silence.

"Is that a yes, or a no?" He asked.

There was a quality in his voice she didn't understand. Was he mocking her? "I meant only that it would take a very long time to teach you. Is that not what I said?"

"Forgive me for teasing you." He answered, trying to keep a straight face. "Levity is a bad habit I have."

"Is that levity?" She asked. "We know so little of it here. We are a solemn people."

"I'm sorry. It may take me some time to get used to being solemn."

"No, forgive me. I could get used to being light

hearted if I felt it wasn't against God's will. We of course, have time for being happy, taking pleasure in the harvest, dancing, but we don't 'tease', as you call it. Marianne did, though. We were close, she and I." They were both silent for a time. "Why did you become a physician?" She asked.

"Well, I think it began with the death of my father. He had cancer and died very quickly. I began wondering then if I should treat humans instead of animals. Then, my nephew, my sister's son, was in a car accident and..."

"A what?"

"A car, I mean, automobile accident." He could feel her confusion. "Well, it's a...it's a carriage, a carriage accident."

"I see." She said doubtfully.

"Anyway, he was hurt badly and the doctor who treated him butchered him so much he lost his leg and nearly died long after he had healed from the accident." He paused. "I decided then that there was more need for a human doctor than an animal one."

"Was it really a carriage?" She asked, frowning prettily.

William laughed into the darkness again. "No," he gained control of himself. "It wasn't a carriage, but it's what we use instead of carriages."

"Is it like a carriage?"

"It's not pulled by horses at all," he answered. "It has an engine that makes it go. You sit inside it with a heater and a radio..." he started laughing again. "No wonder Marianne didn't tell you these things."

Frederick and George joined them on the porch. "Is he telling some of his fantastic tales?" George asked.

"Yes, he is." Diana said soberly. "I believe he is delirious." They all laughed at that. They then talked a little of plans to go back to their people and join in the building of the new community. William was silent while the others made their plans. "Before we leave, I want to take a little time to explore the shack in the village. I have an idea, but I don't want to voice it until I have seen this apparition you describe." Diana asserted.

"Well, at least we know the boys weren't lying, that's something." George said.

"Father Jonathan will be pleased." Frederick observed.

William rose and walked out to the corrals, a shadow in the moonlight.

"What will he do?" Diana asked, watching him walk away from them.

"I think he plans to go with us," George answered.

"Doesn't he want to go back to his own world?"

"I don't know if he can. He was brought here in the fog."

"What does that mean?" Diana asked. "I have lived through many fogs in my lifetime, but you are talking of something else. Will was always talking of this mysterious fog to which you are referring. What is it?"

"Yes," Frederick said soberly. "Yes, we have seen many strange things up beyond the mountains, but always there is a bank of fog or cloud between us and whatever we observe. I never thought of it before now, even though Will Armstrong often spoke of it. This isn't just fog, you're right. It is something else entirely."

"We never understood, did we?" George said.

"No, but Brother Armstrong did. He always knew. He knew exactly what he was doing that day we found the girl, Marianne, too. The flying machine broke through the fog, or brought it to us." They became silent.

"And does William Avery know what you mean?" Diana asked.

Frederick looked out toward the corrals where William stood alone. "He's from the other side of the fog, Sister Macklin." He said quietly. "Somehow, Marianne went to the other side and brought him back with her. He seems to know he is cut off from all he ever knew before. Somehow, it seems to bring him peace."

"I think she brought him to you," George added shyly. "Well, you know, he was very sick, and she knew you could heal him."

"He looks very much like Brother Armstrong."

"Yes, it was frightening at first. We thought we saw a ghost." George laughed lightly.

"He says you remind him of someone he knew on the other side," Frederick said to Diana.

"Anita?" She mused. "When he was delirious, he spoke of both Marianne and Anita." She explained.

"He didn't mention a name, just that you look something like someone he knew." He paused. "Already he speaks as if his former life is over, like a dream."

Marianne got up and walked down to join William. He never looked around as she stepped up beside him, leaning her back against the fence. "Will you go with us, Will?" She caught herself. "I mean, William, Brother Avery."

He smiled. She could see the whiteness of his teeth in the moonlight. "It's fine, Diana. You may call me Will or William." He paused. "Will you teach me about herbs?"

"Do you want to spend a lifetime learning?" She smiled up at him.

William turned to face her, stepping forward until they were almost touching. "Is that a proposal?" He smiled as his left hand came up to grasp her right elbow. Diana frowned at him slightly. He didn't give her time to answer, just swept her into his arms and kissed her before she could catch another breath. Panic seized her and she stiffened, but William was insistent for a moment. He relaxed then, and released her slightly, keeping her close to him. "If I marry you, will you teach me?" He asked.

Diana was dumbfounded. She wanted to shout

for joy, but her entire upbringing didn't allow for either that or the behavior of this man. "I, please let me go, William," she said softly. He dropped his arms from around her. She looked at him, then turned abruptly and walked back to the cabin. She walked between Frederick and George and to her bed where she retired for the night. Not that she slept, but she stayed there, even when she heard the men come in and go to bed, Frederick making a straw bed in the room with George.

"Forgive me, <u>Sister</u> Diana," William whispered from the doorway. But, she didn't respond, just stared at the wall before her. Eventually, she did sleep though, just as morning was lighting the forest. And the men let her sleep until well into midmorning.

She rose quietly, stepping outside the back door to the washstand where she freshened herself and combed her hair. Then, she joined the men on the porch, where she could hear the hum of their subdued voices. "Good morning," she smiled shyly as she stepped out onto the porch.

Frederick and George quickly left for the barn to care for the horses, which were not in need of care.

"You slept long, if not well," William observed.

"I'm rested," she said, settling herself against a post as she sat on the top step of the porch.

"Diana, Sister Macklin, is it?"

She put up a hand to stop him. "I struggled many hours with this, William. I came to the conclusion that you are my destiny as Will felt Marianne was his," she sighed.

"Well, that's romantic," he muttered.

She smiled. "I am getting to know the tone of your levity," she observed. "I do not understand the words, but I know you are teasing me, as you say."

He smiled. "Actually, I was being sarcastic, but I won't try to explain the difference to you all in one day." A mischievous grin made his eyes sparkle. "Will you give me a lifetime to teach you the nuances of the modern language?"

"While I teach you about herbs?" She asked dryly.

"We'll be too busy teaching and learning to make a living, someone will have to support us."

Now it was Diana's turn to laugh. It felt good to let out her innermost feelings. *This is what true happiness feels like,* she thought, but suppressed it quickly. "Tell me, William," she began. "Why do you speak of marriage to a woman you met only a few days ago?"

"That is a fair question," he observed. "When I first awoke, I thought you were my old friend, Anita Wallick, a nurse I worked with and dated for several years. You resemble her."

"Do you love her?"

He considered for a moment. "I suppose I felt we would someday marry, but someday never seemed to come around. Now, I know why." He smiled at her, and she imagined she could see love from his eyes. He continued. "While you resemble Anita, Diana, you are not her and I know it. You may be right, perhaps destiny is a good word." He paused. "Did I love Anita? Perhaps. But, Diana, I am <u>in</u> love with you! I know that, too, even after only a few days."

Diana stared at him. There it was, all the things she dreamed of hearing Will say to her were being said by William. *He makes me laugh and feel...what do I feel?* She frowned slightly. *Is this truly love? It's not the comfortable, long friendship that Will and I shared. William experienced that with his friend, too.* She smiled shyly at William, who was watching her closely. "We'll see, William. When we get home, we'll see."

He nodded in answer.

They hadn't noticed Frederick and George come back to the cabin. "We should be heading back to the people," Frederick said. He smiled broadly at Diana and William, his face reddening a little at what he'd heard.

Diana turned to them, her face radiating her happiness without her realizing it. At the looks of expectancy on their faces she blushed slightly, but shook it off. She was too happy to be embarrassed now. "First, I want to go down to the village and look for...whatever I find." She said.

"I'll go with her," William offered.

She looked at him, in thoughtful acceptance. "I think that would be good," she said. "Marianne, or whoever is down there won't be shy of him, either because she knows him or because she doesn't, and maybe won't hide from us. I hope not, at least."

"Don't go into the fog," Frederick said.

"We won't," William stepped forward as he spoke. Diana looked up at him as he approached her. He offered her a hand to stand up from the step where she was seated.

She watched as her small hand became one with his larger hand, fitting as though it had always known its place. Her heart and mind soared with the joy she felt. *At last, my life will be fulfilled.* She thought. *Thank you, Marianne. Thank you, wherever you are! Whoever you are!*

Six

Out of Shadow and Ashes

George prepared the horses for them, then William and Diana rode down the hill to the village. They put their horses in the corral, hastily fixing it to hold them temporarily. Diana led the way right to the door of the little shack. It wasn't locked, but no one was inside, which came as no surprise. William looked around the clearing and peeked into the barn, then joined Diana as she walked around the root cellar and into the trees beyond. They walked silently to a small burned-out clearing, but found no one there. Diana turned and looked thoughtfully back the way they had come, up into the blackened trees, then into the remnant of the forest. "Rachel!" She called softly. "Rachel!" Now, more loudly.

"There are some small footprints over here near this old tree," William observed quietly.

Diana nodded absently. She walked slowly back to the root cellar and then into the ruins of the barn. William lingered in the forest behind her, but followed after only a few moments.

"Rachel!" Diana said again. A sound from the shadows near the entrance of the barn caused her to spin around and look under the ruined bench. "Oh, Rachel!" She breathed. "It is you, isn't it?"

"Diana?" Came the raspy whisper.

"Yes!" Diana rushed to take the girl into her arms.

"Don't look at me!" Hissed the girl as she struggled to cover her head with her cloak.

William appeared in the entrance and bent low to help Diana with the struggling girl. He held a firm hand against her back until she finally relaxed against Diana's shoulder, her face hidden in the hollow of Diana's neck. The hood of the cloak was up over her head, but both Diana and William had seen enough to be sickened by the scars and injuries.

"Rachel, look at me," Diana cajoled. "We already have seen most of your face, now look at me. It's all right, My Darling. We're here to help you. You aren't alone anymore."

"We can't help you, Child, until we can see the damage." William said softly, patting over her head hidden in the cloak.

"Who is that?" Came the whispered reply. "It can't be Brother Armstrong, I know it can't!" She snuggled deeper into Diana's shoulder.

Diana and William smiled at one another. "Oh, Rachel, Rachel!" Diana crooned as she rocked the girl. "We were told you were dead, did you know that?"

Rachel nodded vigorously against Diana's shoulder.

"Oh, My Dear Child, what have you been through?" Diana was crying, and she could feel Rachel's sobs through the thinness of her clothing.

"I wish I died," Rachel mourned.

"Oh! No, Rachel!" Diana pried the girl away from her. Rachel sat up, but kept her face well hidden.

William tried to move the hood away from Rachel's face, but she seemed to crumple away from him within the cloth. "Who is he?" She whispered.

Diana peered under the edge of the hood. She could see Rachel looking out at her. "It is you!" She smiled at the girl. "I see you in there!" Rachel quickly looked down. "His name is William, Brother Avery. He's a physician and I've brought him here to help you."

"No!" Rachel shrunk even farther under the cloth, if possible.

Diana changed tactics. "Did you build that room onto the root cellar by yourself?"

Rachel nodded, but offered nothing else.

"Well, you did a good job. But, don't you want to come home with us, now? Home, where we can love you and heal you?"

"At your house?" Rachel whispered.

"Well, no, Dear, not exactly." Diana said. "We're building a new village. You could come there and live with us. Uncle Edward is there, waiting."

Rachel's head started shaking before Diana

finished. "No, no..."

"Rachel, we can't leave you here, alone," Diana pleaded. "We will be several days away. You can't stay here alone."

"Mother's with me," she answered.

Diana frowned up at William who mouthed and gestured to her. "There's no one else here."

"Rachel, you know your mother died when you were only a baby," Diana answered.

"No, my new mother," Rachel hissed.

Diana frowned again, then asked. "Do you mean Marianne?"

Rachel nodded vigorously.

"Has she been here with you?"

"I've seen her," Rachel offered.

"Yes, well, she has led Diana and I here to help you," William said softly, crouching down to be near Diana. "It was Marianne who brought me here to this valley. I think she wants me to try to help you."

Rachel raised her head slightly. Diana, seated on her left could plainly see the left side of Rachel's face. It looked so normal, if a little thin and haggard. Fresh tears flooded her already streaked face.

William could only see the damaged right side of Rachel's face, the protruding eye, the ridged and scarred face and head. He knew she meant for him to see, hoping that he would be horrified. He reached out and removed the cloak so he could see the knob of her ear and the further damage to her head. It was horrible, yes, but the doctor in him responded to the needed care. He laid a hand on her shoulder. "Let us help you, Rachel. I think I can." He said.

Rachel turned her head to see him better. Defiance was in her left eye. "What can you do with that?" She demanded in her hoarse whisper, a hand waving up at her face.

Diana reached out and turned Rachel's head so she could see what William was seeing. She had watched his face as his jaw tightened and she knew he was fighting emotional upheaval. But, she wasn't prepared for what she observed. "Oh, Rachel!" She breathed.

Rachel hurriedly put the cloak back up over her head, scrabbling away from Diana.

"Can't you talk, Child?" William asked gently. "There's no need to whisper, so tell me what happened to your throat. I don't see more than superficial burn scars to the side of your neck. Can you tell me what happened? Is there other damage that I can't see?"

"Are these all burn scars?" Diana asked. William nodded. "Rachel, were you in the house when it burned down? Couldn't you get out? Were you trapped inside there?" She looked out the doorway toward the embers and ashes that had once been the Stuart home.

"No, Diana, these are old scars." William waved a hand at her, still looking at Rachel, hidden inside her cloak. "The town fires were too recent to have done this. There's no redness, no soot."

"She choked me," Rachel whimpered in her

curious whisper.

William looked askance at Diana.

"Who do you mean, Sarah?" Diana queried of the girl.

"The Witch!" Rachel spat out defiantly. "But, she's dead now. She won't ever hurt anybody again."

"Sarah did this to you? She did something to your throat?" Diana asked in mounting horror. "Rachel, surely you don't mean she burned you, too?"

"Who's Sarah?" William asked.

Diana looked at him, shock registering in her face. "Her grandmother, my aunt. But, Rachel's right, she is dead." She turned to Rachel. "Did you see her, when Marianne killed her?" Diana asked.

"Mother didn't do that," Rachel sobbed, folding herself into her own lap. Her sobs were deep and her shoulders heaved with the force of her crying.

Diana scooted over to her and put her arms around Rachel, crying with her. William left them alone. We walked outside and looked more closely at the shelter Rachel had built. He marveled that the girl could have done such a good job with only one eye and limited strength. He wondered about the history of this place and what he had gotten into. *I've got to know more about these people,* he thought. *If I am here to help them, I've got to know their history as well as the present.* He sighed deeply. He was still fatigued, himself. He looked around the area, but could see no fog, the sun was shining bright from a blue, blue sky. He could see the devastation fire had caused to the little village. He walked to the broken down corral, then methodically made some more permanent repairs so it would hold the horses more securely. Though smaller than it used to be, it could still be used to hold an animal or two without worry. He unsaddled their horses and turned them loose once again into the tiny enclosure.

There was a water trough, but it was dry. He found the pump for a well, about half way between the burned out house and the barn. When he tried to make it work, he became frustrated with his efforts. He got water from the shelter and primed and pumped, then took the pump apart and removed the old, cracked leather. He put the leathers into the bucket of water to soften it up, massaging the water into the fibers. His work paid off. When he put the pump back together and primed it once again, he could hear the gurgling liquid coming up and soon was rewarded with water splashing onto the stones at his feet. "She'll have to keep it primed and use it everyday," he commented as Diana joined him.

"I put her to bed in her little room, there," Diana nodded toward the shack.

"I saw you cross the dooryard," he said. "I thought it best to not interfere.

"I don't know how to help her," Diana mourned.

"Do you know how old she is?" He asked.

"Oh, I would say fourteen or sixteen seasons. It must be that long since Ruth, her mother died."

"Why do you say seasons and not years?" He asked, frowning.

"It's just our way," she shrugged. "Does it matter?"

"No." He shook his head. "Help me take water to the horses, there." He pointed to the corral. For a little while they quietly worked together, walking back and forth with buckets of water, dumping them into the trough, then filling them and doing it all over again. Then William broke their silence. "Diana, I don't have the equipment or medication required to help her, either." He said sadly.

"What do you mean?" She asked. "The e...e-kwip..."

"Equipment, tools; the things I would need to do surgery on her face." He explained as though she had any idea what he was saying.

"William, I don't understand. You mean, her face could be fixed?" She looked incredulously at him. "How?"

"It's a surgical procedure, Diana." He explained. "They do it all the time. Actually, she probably doesn't need reconstruction, just skin grafts and..." He sighed. "I don't have the tools to do it."

"What tools? What do you need?"

He let out a long, slow breath. "I don't even have my medical bag. I don't have the most primitive of doctor's tools."

"Is that the bag under the bed?"

"What bag? Is my backpack under the bed in the

cabin?" His face was wreathed in joy. "Marianne brought my backpack along? Ha-ha! I didn't know I had it with me!" He pulled her to him and hugged her tightly.

"I'm not sure what a back pack is," Diana answered, pulling away from him. "But, there is a blue and black bag of some kind, with small cords tied to it and a..."

"That's it!" He cried, letting her go.

"I'm sure Frederick and George will bring it with them when they join us tomorrow," she said. "Does it have the things you need?"

"It did have my medical bag in it when we started out." He nodded in confirmation. "I hope it still does. That means I'm still a doctor. I still have the means to help people."

"And you can fix Rachel's face?"

"I'm not sure how much I can do there." He frowned into the sunlight. "I just don't know, Diana. I could try. I don't have a lot of the tools I would need, but I do have some things. I might be able to improvise. I do have the knowledge to do it." He paused just a moment, a frown creasing his brow. "I wish I had a few manuals with me, too."

"You're used to such a different world," she said quietly.

He took both of her hands in his and looked directly into her upturned face. "You're right, I am. But, not everyone in my modern world gets the opportunity to be a pioneer in the true sense of the word. Many desire it, or think they do, but no one ever gets to do it. You have no idea how exhilarating it is for me."

"Does that mean you're happy?" She asked with a slight smile.

He laughed. "Now, look who's teasing." He pulled her to him and rocked her back and forth. Her arms went naturally around him and felt comfortable there. Diana closed her eyes, a smile playing first at the corners of her mouth, then spreading to infuse her whole face. "Does this mean you will consider marrying me?" He asked, suddenly sounding serious.

Diana pulled back and looked at him. "First, we'll need to see what Uncle Edward thinks of you." She said.

"Why, will I be marrying him as well?"

She poked him in the side. "No. But, he will be living with us. He's my mother's brother and has lived with me most of my adult life."

"So, in effect I will be marrying him, too."

"Well..." He cut off her response by kissing her. This time, she kissed him back. It was a joyful thing. She felt breathless as he finally pulled away.

"I won't have to kiss him too, will I?" He asked, looking at her innocently.

She blushed. "Oh, William!" She hid her face in his shirt, for a moment, then pulled away, hands on hips. "What can we do for Rachel?" She asked, feigning sternness. "You've completely sidestepped our conversation!"

"Why?" William smiled disarmingly at her. "Will she be living with us, too?"

"Perhaps!" She said, a smile betraying her. "William, please, be serious. She needs help."

"That she does." He answered. "First of all, I think with the horses we could pull some of that debris off the barn and make her a better house out of the remaining structure. It would be tighter and much more secure. There's enough wood to put in a floor and there's already a heater in it."

"You can't mean to leave her here? I, I was talking about fixing her face."

"Do you think she'll go with us right now?" He shook his head. "I think the minute Fred and George show up, she'll go into hiding again. She doesn't want anyone to see her. She isn't ready to change her world, right now."

"Does he know you call him Fred?" Diana asked, momentarily distracted.

"Who?" He frowned. "That's his name, isn't it?"

"Well, Frederick, yes," she nodded absently.

"He hasn't corrected me."

"Hm-m-m-m," she answered. They were silent for a moment. "I thought you said you could fix Rachel's face?" She frowned. "Didn't you?"

"I'm not sure if fix is the right word. I might be able to make some changes. What I can fix, with Fred and George's help, is her surroundings. If she is fourteen or fifteen years old, she can survive on her own with food, water, and shelter. Even in her pain, she has managed pretty well."

"But, we'll be days and days away. Winter will set in and she'll be alone, and..."

"And we'll visit her as often as possible until she is comfortable enough to be with others. I'll do what I can for her, but it may not seem like much."

"Poor, poor Rachel." Diana crooned, looking back at the tiny cabin.

"She doesn't need that kind of pity, Diana." He directed. "I'm much more worried about her emotional scarring than the physical, although that's bad enough. Whatever has happened to her, she needs to talk that out, and she needs to feel useful and resourceful for herself. If we help her too much, like taking her home and seeing to her every need, she will become an emotional disaster. She is a very mature teenager, now, with the unsolved emotional issues of a child. And those of an adult, if I'm reading this right. She needs to be on her own, with what medical help and emotional guidance we can afford her."

Diana stared at him. "I have no idea what you just said. Well, that's not quite true, but I don't understand most of it. You mean to leave her here, that's obvious."

"Yes."

"But, you also want to try to help her with her face, is that right?"

"While you help her with her emotional problems.

She's obviously been through more than anyone should be expected to endure. She needs you to talk her through that."

"And we're to do all this within the next, say, few days?"

"Right."

"And then just leave her here?"

"She won't go, Diana. It will all work out. Trust me, I'm not sure of the details, but I do know it will work out for the best."

Diana turned around and walked away. She was mumbling to herself. "He can't mean this," she muttered. "He's crazy and I've been entertaining ideas of loving him," she sighed and shook her head. Diana looked in on Rachel who was sleeping. She looked at the food storage in the cellar and marveled at the work Rachel must have done to provide water and shelter for herself. "Well, the pump is working now, so that will ease her load," she said. That stopped her dead in her tracks. "What am I saying? I'm talking as if all the crazy things William says are true!" She shook her head and kept walking, to the barn, to the corrals, anywhere but to face him again for a while.

She needn't have worried. William had walked off into the village to look at anything they could possibly use to help Rachel build a better shelter. "I know I'm right!" He muttered. "Somehow this is all going to turn out all right."

"Thank you, Dr. Avery." Came a voice from behind a shed to his right.

He stepped closer to see her better. "Marianne," he said with finality. "Don't you think it's time to let these good people see you and quit playing these games?"

She smiled. "They don't need me anymore. They have you."

"I don't know if I can fulfill that legacy."

"You can." She encouraged. "You have already brought joy to Dear Diana and will yet bring Rachel back to life. That's all I've ever really cared about."

"Where's your fogbank?" He looked around them at the brightness of the day.

"Sometime, you may understand that," she said. "But, for now, you are the catalyst that will bring them to their destiny."

"Then, I <u>am</u> right. It will all turn out all right."

"It is your turn to bring them all from the shadows into the light." She said.

He would have answered her, but she stepped behind the shed and, he supposed, walked on into the forest. "Or into oblivion," he muttered. He understood her reticence when he heard footsteps behind him and turned to face Diana.

"Are you hungry? I've made a kind of stew from the stores in the root cellar. Rachel's awake."

"Yes!" He said emphatically, holding out a hand for her. As they walked away, he glanced behind the shed, but saw no one, nor did he really expect to.

After they ate, Rachel let William look at her scars. "The eye will be easy to fix." He declared.

"Really?" Diana asked with interest. Although still terrible, it was getting easier to look objectively at Rachel's ruined flesh.

"Well, we can do one of two things," he explained. "We can take the eyeball out and stitch the lid closed permanently, or we can push it back and take a couple of stitches here, and here," he demonstrated. "To keep the eyeball back where it should be. Infection will be the worst thing to worry about. If it does become infected we may have to remove it, anyway."

Rachel's left eye watered profusely. "Don't take my eye away," she whispered.

"Okay," he answered, smiling reassuringly. "For now, it stays. Can you see at all out of it?" He waved his hand in front of her.

"Only shadows," she answered, closing her eyes. The lid on the right eye didn't quite cover the protruding eyeball.

"Did you see me just waving at you?"

"No," she said, her head down.

He turned to Diana. "Most of this scarring on her face will heal in time, leaving a redness, well, because it's scar tissue, but it's the eye that attracts attention. When we fix that, the rest will seem not so bad."

"But, these ridges here," Diana pointed out. "And her ear."

"Can you hear through this ear, Rachel?" He whispered close to the knob on the right side of her head.

"Yes," she answered.

"Then," he gently manipulated the protruding skin. "Then, I think I can flatten this out so it doesn't look so bad, but it will never look like the other one. I cannot do intricate plastic surgery here in this wilderness."

Diana and Rachel both starred at him for a moment, trying to take in what he was saying. "But, her hair will cover it better if it's flattened." Diana offered. "If we comb it over this way," she demonstrated. "Her natural hair is so thick you can almost not see the gray underneath. And I think the ear will be completely covered."

"Time will do a lot, Diana," he answered, as he looked at Rachel's hand. "I can clip here between her fingers so she is more mobile," he said. That's about all she needs there. The arm will heal and look better as time passes." He smiled at Rachel who ducked her head in embarrassment. He felt her throat and had her talk to him as best she could. "Somehow her larynx and vocal cords have been damaged."

"What does that mean?" Diana asked.

William took her hand and placed two fingers on his own throat. "These are your vocal cords. They vibrate when you talk. It's what makes you have sound." He placed her fingers on Rachel's throat. "Speak a few words, Rachel." He said gently.

She looked at Diana. "I, I love you, Diana," she whispered.

Tears streamed down both their faces as they collapsed in one another's arms until they gained their composure.

"I can't tell you what kind of pressure it takes to do this much damage to a throat." He felt again. "Did you feel the difference, Diana, between her throat and mine?" He massaged Rachel's throat for a moment. "Does it hurt at all, Rachel?"

"Only when you push on it," she answered.

He sat back, nodding. "Someone nearly choked her to death. Did they use a rope or ligature of any kind?" He asked.

Rachel frowned at him, then spoke to Diana. "She choked me because she thought I had been talking to you or Mother through my boarded up window."

"She did this with her hands?" He asked. Rachel nodded. "Whew!" He let out a sudden breath. "She obviously had the strength of the insane," he observed dryly. "How did she burn your head and arm, Child?" He asked.

"I had disobeyed. She..." Rachel looked up at Diana, pleading for understanding with her good eye. "She pushed me onto the stove." She swallowed hard. "I hit her with my arm and pushed myself away from the stove with my other hand." She held her damaged hand before her, staring at it.

"Oh, Rachel, I'm so sorry!" Diana cried. They held each other then, and William left the room. He busied himself with work on the barn. He hated seeing carnage of any kind, but on a child, it bothered him most of all. Diana didn't follow him, so he just kept working. It helped ease his frustration while he waited for his instruments to arrive.

Frederick Wilder and George Bays actually arrived in time for supper that very day. They were amazed that Rachel was their mysterious apparition. She wouldn't let them see her, and they didn't push the issue. William explained the problems with the girl. They, in turn, explained some things to him about the history of their village and the indomitable Sarah Stuart. They were interested in William's project with the barn. It was something they could understand and feel fulfilled in doing. After a good night's sleep, they started on that project.

William was not disappointed in the contents of his backpack. In the early morning light, he pulled out each item almost reverently. There was a change of clothes, a sleeping bag, and a mess kit. In the very bottom of the pack, lay his medical bag. He pulled it out reverently and let the backpack drop to the ground, then set the black bag next to it. "Pioneer," he mumbled to himself. "You always wanted to be a pioneer. Now, you can be a pioneer in medicine." He knelt on the ground and opened the bag, looking lovingly at the familiar tools and medicines. It wasn't much, but it would do. With the contents of this bag and some ingenuity, he could build up a practice among this primitive people and help them. He had modern knowledge and with even his limited technology, he could not only cure them of their ills, but utterly amaze them. Ironically, he realized that the medicines to cure his pneumonia had been with him all along. He looked up at the brightening sky. *Whatever the plan is for me, it has to do with this primitive people,* he thought. *Good-bye, Anita.*

He thought of his childhood and the days he spent pretending to be a cowboy or a pioneer, walking across the wilderness with a covered wagon train. He looked again into the open medical bag. *Now, here I am,* he mused. *Living out my fantasy.* He shook his head in amazement.

Diana watched William open his belongings. At the look on his face, she felt embarrassed that she had intruded into what was obviously a deep, personal moment. Her heart filled with love at his tenderness, and tears spilled down her cheeks. She started to back away, but he looked up at the movement. Tears filled his own eyes and spilled over. He held out a hand to her and she went to him, sitting down on the ground next to him. She peered into the bag in open awe. "Tell me about these tools," she said softly.

William laid a small towel on his backpack and laid the tools upon it, telling Diana the name of each of them and a brief description of what could be done with them.

She sat in stunned silence, looking at the foreign objects before her. She had always been confident in her abilities to heal with herbs and the knowledge passed on to her by her mother. She could successfully set broken bones and mend cuts and deep wounds.

Now, she felt small in comparison to the knowledge and technology laid before her. She had no doubt he could do what he said, but it seemed incomprehensible to her. "You say you cut people open deliberately, then fix them inside?" She shook her head in wonder. "How do they stand the pain of such a thing?"

William smiled at her naivety. "Well, I put them under. That is, an anaesthesiologist does that for me." He grinned at her raised eyebrows and doubtful look. "It is something we'll have to work on, isn't it?" He said. "I have a little ether, but I'll have to think long about how to render a patient unconscious for surgery, now."

Diana stared at him. She couldn't quite grasp all he was saying, but... "I know of some herbs that will make a person sleep deeply, but I don't know if they could feel the kind of pain you would inflict upon them." She shook her head in wonder. "You won't do any of this to Rachel, will you?"

"No," he quickly reassured her. "Rachel needs only cosmetic surgery, but it will be painful. She will need to be under..." He laughed at the look of bewilderment on her face. "Don't make me explain that." He said.

She was speechless. She simply shook her head and said nothing. William packed up his belongings, then they walked to the barn where George and Frederick had made considerable progress at making the ruins look like a dwelling. Inside, there were three small rooms and a loft for sleeping or storage. Diana was impressed, but saddened at what this could mean. She didn't want to leave Rachel behind them.

They ate a midday meal together, after moving most of Rachel's belongings into her new quarters. Rachel didn't join them, but insisted on hiding in the root cellar. After the meal, Diana coaxed Rachel out into the dooryard where William waited to work on her injuries. He and the other men had fashioned an adequate operating table. There, in the bright sunlight of a perfect day, he, with Diana assisting, did what they could to repair the marred flesh, the tortured eye, and the disfigured ear. Diana had herbs that caused slumber and William had his small amount of ether. They combined their healing arts to bring about what they hoped would be a miracle for Rachel. It took nearly all of William's bandaging to cover the wounds when they were done. Only time would tell now, what would happen. "We won't know for several days if it is going to heal as I hope," he told Diana and a groggy Rachel.

Diana stayed with their patient while the men repaired more of the fences and made the new 'home' ever better. When Diana emerged from the crude room where Rachel lay healing, on the following day, the men were poring over a small cart they had found under the barn debris. It was mostly intact and usable with only minor repairs. Those they dispatched with quickly. "We can leave a horse for Rachel and use this cart to carry a couple of us," Frederick was saying. "Then, when she's ready to join us, she can ride home within a few days."

"There's still a lot of usable hay in the back, there," George explained. "She'll do fine for a few months, if need be."

"We do need to be going, though. Our people need us to build homes and take care of them for the coming winter. I don't know what we'll do for feed." Frederick mopped at his perspiring brow.

"I'll stay behind with Rachel for a few more days," said Diana. "I don't want to leave her until she feels much better."

"I'll stay as well," William spoke up. "You know the way to the new village, am I right?" He asked her.

"Yes," she nodded.

It was agreed then. The cart was left for Diana and William and an extra horse for Rachel, if need be. The two friends headed for their new home on the following morning, leaving Rachel with Diana and William. "Uncle Edward will worry, but please try to explain everything to him," Diana instructed before they left. "He'll be so relieved to hear that our Rachel is alive."

"We'll tell him," answered Frederick. "Not many would believe us, so we will tell only Edward and Father Jonathan what we have found here. Then we will wait for you to come."

"If you don't return soon, we'll come back looking," added George as they mounted and rode away.

Diana and William watched them go, then turned their attention to their patient. She was awake and able to eat. She couldn't get enough water to drink. "The ether makes you dry," William explained. "She'll level off soon." Diana looked pensive, causing William to laugh. "She'll be fine. This is normal."

"Thank you," she curtsied slightly.

William shook his head, smiling at Diana. *Life with this woman is going to be perfect,* he thought. *She is so completely guileless and lovely. What have I done to deserve this opportunity?*

Diana smiled back at him, then turned to watch Rachel. *He's so wonderful and kind and patient with me,* she thought. *I wonder why the Lord is blessing me so well.*

Rachel giggled. She looked first at Diana and then at William, then back at Diana and giggled again. It was raspy, but still made them smile at her. It was the first time she had shown any joy at all.

"I feel like laughing, myself," Diana whispered. Rachel nodded knowingly.

William shook his head, but he was smiling, too. "You can get up, Rachel. The more you exercise and return to a normal routine, the faster you will heal."

"No..." Diana started. "She needs to rest and heal."

"Not true," he answered. "It was proven long ago that getting back to normal as quickly as possible promotes the healing, not the other way round."

Diana frowned. "Long ago?"

"Well," he scratched his head. "Long ago in my history, perhaps in the future for you. Like, starting now." With that, he walked out, waiting for no more argument.

"He likes you," Rachel commented.

"I believe he does." Diana nodded, looking after him, out the open door.

Rachel felt up over the bandages on her head with her good hand. "Did you help him do this?" She asked.

"I did." Diana assured her. "It was a remarkable thing. He is very gifted."

"Can he fix my voice?"

"No. He says time will heal you and it will get better, but never back to what it was before."

"Oh."

"It will just make you a very soft spoken woman."

Rachel smiled sadly.

"Rachel, I've been thinking about the fires and the destruction here," she indicated the valley with the sweep of her arm. "I believe there is a purpose for it all."

"I want to sleep now, Diana," Rachel said, scooting back down into her bedding. "I don't want to talk."

Diana adjusted the bedding, then walked outside into the gathering dusk. The air still smelled faintly of soot, but it was a bright, clear evening with a beautiful sunset causing the mountains to glow with a soft pink light. She saw William walking down beyond the corrals and turned in that direction to be with him. He smiled when she reached him and silently took her arm and hand into his, pressing her arm close to his side, as they walked along the deserted road. "Do you have regrets, Will?" She asked. "About leaving your other life?"

He stopped and looked at her. *Do I?* He wondered. *Do I miss the traffic and hubbub of the modern world?* He smiled down at her. "No," he said. "I am somehow perfectly at home, wherever I am." He paused. "As long as I am with you."

She had no answer to that, only a smile. It was something she never would have heard from the lips of Will Armstrong. She wondered idly if he ever said pretty things to Marianne. She knew they talked much more than she and Will had, about personal things. She and William continued walking to the end of the road where the creek ran under a crude bridge and a footpath wandered into the forest. They stood looking at the rushing water. The creek babbled and spoke to them of life and hope and joy, a continuing of the course of the world. They absorbed the message of healing into their own hearts. As they turned to walk back to the house, William suddenly quoted scripture to her. "Yea, though I walk through the valley of the shadow of death, I will fear no evil; for thou art with me."

"The valley of the shadow of death," Diana breathed. "The valley of pain, of soot and ashes."

"When we leave here," William half whispered.

"I want only to leave the shadows, the soot, and the ashes. There should be no more pain here, or evil."

Diana smiled as she laid her head against his arm. "Yes!" She answered fervently.

The following day, William removed the bandaging from Rachel's head. There was only a little bruising around her eye and ear.

"Oh, Rachel!" Diana exclaimed. "There is so much difference already!"

"Really?"

"Oh, yes!"

"It's going to heal nicely," William commented. He covered her eye again. "Not time to leave that open to the elements." He said. "We don't want too much light all at once and we don't want any infections setting in."

Diana had Rachel feel her tender flesh. The ridges were gone, replaced by a smoother feeling skin, though tender. She gingerly touched her new ear. It felt almost like the other one, but smaller. She felt them both, tears streaming down her face. She looked at her hand. The black stitches between her fingers weren't pretty, but her fingers were separated again and it made her smile, and cry. "Mother," she sobbed. "Look, Mother!"

"Why do you call Marianne Mother?" Diana asked, sitting next to Rachel.

Rachel looked away.

"Here, let me comb your hair, let's get you bathed, then we'll go for a walk and maybe talk a little bit."

Diana warmed some water for bathing and then helped Rachel clean herself. There was a clean dress on a shelf and Diana helped her into it. Then, she washed and combed, and trimmed Rachel's hair, drawing it over to the right side of her head. As she hoped, it covered the scarring and the gray hair and baldness caused by her injuries. "You look like a new woman!" She exclaimed. "You've grown up so much. You're not our little Rachel anymore. You really are a woman, now."

Rachel ducked her head in embarrassment. But, she was pleased.

They walked arm in arm to Rachel's favorite place in the burned out forest. "It used to be so pretty here," she whispered. "I used to sit under this tree." She put a hand on the blackened tree trunk.

"You used to hide treasures in it, too." Diana said softly.

"How did you know?" Rachel whirled to face her friend. "I thought it was my secret place!" She pouted.

"A long time ago, Elias told me. He said he brought you here and told you it could be your own special place. Do you remember that?"

Rachel nodded, tears springing to her eye and washing down her face. "Grandfather..." She whispered wistfully.

"He loved you so much, Rachel."

"I know. Everyone who loved me died."

"Oh, no Rachel! I love you and I'm still here."

Diana rushed to the girl and took her sobbing into her arms where she rocked her for some time before she was calm.

"Was it my fault that my parents died, Diana? And grandfather?" Rachel asked suddenly.

"No, Rachel. It wasn't your fault at all. Why would you think that?"

"Grandmother..." her hoarse whisper trailed off.

"Did she tell you it was your fault? Did she blame you for the evil she did herself?"

Rachel nodded. "I killed her. In the red glow of those fires, I killed her."

"Oh, Rachel!" Diana held her even tighter.

"She killed me and I killed her. Now, no one else needs to die. It's over." She said it matter- of-factly, as if she were detached from the words.

"Rachel, you are not dead," Diana said firmly. "You are very much alive, and no matter what happened here, you're right, it is over. You needn't torture yourself with this."

Rachel stood in the circle of Diana's arms in a stupor. She showed no emotion now, just a calm resignation that was more frightening than her tears or her confessions. Diana turned her and started walking back to the house. William had moved everything into the new house and Diana took Rachel there and put her to bed. She closed her eyes and seemed to sleep.

"She's begun to talk to me," Diana told William as they sat on a bench he had fashioned in the dooryard.

"We should have just taken this child from Sarah when she was a baby." She shook her head at a flood of memories. "That's what the Smith's wanted to do, and then they died, too. Oh, my!"

Rachel ate and drank, slept and walked, but for two days she didn't say a word. William uncovered her eye and removed all the stitches from her surgeries. Diana had her look at herself in a pool of water. The reflection caused no reaction in her. William assured her that the bruising and scarring would be minimal, and although she would always bear the mark of burned flesh, she would be closer to normal in time.

As they ate supper on the second night, William began a conversation. "Diana," he said. "Tell me the story of the Stuart family."

She looked at him with a frown, but met only his kind smile. She nodded and began. "I don't know too much of their history. My uncle could tell so much more of that. The Stuart's were my mother's people. Elias, my mother's brother, was a kindly man. He married Sarah Macklin. She was a hard hearted girl and an even more offense woman. I don't know what made her so bitter and evil, her brothers and my mother were such kind people." She paused, looking at Rachel who sat at the table eating as though she were alone.

"Did Sarah and Elias have children?" William prodded.

Diana nodded. "Yes, they had a son, Elijah."

Rachel looked up at Diana for the first time.

Diana went on, looking kindly at the girl. "Elijah was a wonderful boy! He was fun and handsome and skilled at the lathe. He worked with his father and helped others all the time. When Elijah was alive, everyone was happy, I think." She paused briefly again, stirring her food with a fork. "He fell in love with a young girl, Ruth Smith. She was so pretty and sweet. She had flowing, black hair tied neatly into a bun, when it would stay. She was small, like Rachel, here. They were a good match, she and Elijah. Her family owned the mill." She stopped, looking up at William with pleading in her eyes. *I can't go on with this,* she thought. He smiled encouragingly. Diana swallowed hard and laid down her fork. "They were married in the springtime. They wanted to live in a little cottage up at the mill, but..."

"Grandmother killed them." Rachel said quietly. "Why didn't she kill me?"

"Your grandfather wouldn't allow it." Diana said. "He kept you alive so there would be hope for his family to go on. You were his pride and joy. He lived because of you."

"Then she killed him!" she cried plaintively. "Why didn't she kill me?"

"Her depravity was full at that time." William offered. "If she got rid of you, she would have no one to vent her anger on except herself. So, she tortured you because she hated herself."

Silence filled the cabin. No one moved to eat or

to leave, they just sat there together, not talking, only thinking.

Rachel broke the silence with her quiet whisper. "She came upon me on the road. The village was burning, everyone was running away. She said she'd killed Mother, but I knew it was a lie. No one could kill Mother. She had a knife in her hand with blood on it. She tried to stab me, but I grabbed her hand and then she tripped. I tried to get away, but she pushed at me again and the knife went into her and she fell on the road. I pushed her into the ravine and ran away into the darkness. I fell into the river, then swam to the other side."

Silence filled the room once again. Tears were flooding Diana's face, but Rachel just sat staring at her empty plate. William watched her for a moment. "Rachel," he finally said. "What you did was in self defense. Even the Lord allows us to defend ourselves."

Diana was nodding in agreement, but she couldn't speak in the emotion of the moment. She cleared her throat once, then again as she got control of herself. "Everyone in the village knew of Sarah's evil, but there was never any proof of her crimes until this moment. She only confessed these things to you and then accused you because she was going to kill you in the end, too. Perhaps she would have even killed herself when everyone else was dead."

"She thought I was going to burn up in the house," Rachel mused. "She locked me in when she left. She was surprised to find me on the road. I was going to Mother and she knew it. She got so mad!" She looked up at her friends. "I didn't mean to kill her, but she..." Again her whispers trailed off.

"I don't think you did kill her," William said. "It sounds to me like she killed herself, after all."

The two women looked at him thoughtfully. "Thank you," Diana mouthed.

He winked at her, then turned to smile kindly at Rachel.

"That's what Mother told me," Rachel responded. "But, I didn't believe her."

"You've talked with Marianne?" Diana asked with interest.

Rachel nodded. "She comes to me sometimes, now." She answered.

"In the fog?" Asked William.

Rachel smiled and nodded. "Sometimes." She said.

"Rachel," Diana began. "We're going to go to our new village. Let's all go soon."

"I can't leave Mother." Rachel didn't look up, just toyed with her fork, pushing a few remnants of food around on her dish.

"Your mother will let you go with us," William said.

Rachel shook her head. "No," she answered simply.

"She let me go," he countered.

"Because she knew you would have Diana," she

answered back. "There is no one for me."

"There could be, now, Rachel." Diana pleaded. "You are going to heal physically and mentally into a lovely person."

"No," Rachel smiled sadly at them. "I am a part of this valley. I'll just stay here with Mother." Finally, she looked up. "You can go."

"Rachel," William said. "The fires have purged this valley of all the evil and hatred of the past. We, Diana and I, have come to take you out of the shadow and the ashes of those fires." He stopped to look at Diana. "We have taken you from the ashes and healed your body. Please, let us take you from the shadow of the past. We want to take you home with us."

Diana looked in amazement at William. Love shone on her face and was answered by the light in his eyes as he gazed back at her.

Rachel looked up at the two people before her. She loved them both. She thought back to the last conversation she'd had with Mother. *'I must soon go away,'* Mother had said. *'You must go on with the living. You have drawn me back to be with you, but I couldn't protect your mortal body. Now is the time for you to live. Let me go on to the land of the shadows.'*

Now, before her sat these two dear people, telling her the same things. *What am I to do?* She thought. "Out of shadow and ashes," she said, then shook her head. "No, not yet, not yet."

Seven

Into the Light

Thomas Woodslee led his little group into the bright sunshine of the verdant mountain valley. A narrow road led down the face of the escarpment on the west side of the valley, to the southern end. A bend in the river made a large inlet just a few hundred feet from their newly-budding home sites. There, they found four cabins almost completed and two more started. There were small barns for each new home, with corrals. He nodded to himself. He lived among a good and generous people. This new group would be welcomed just as he'd said.

Father Jonathan, on his old mule, rode up beside Thomas. "It looks like we were expected," smiled the aging monk.

Thomas nodded. They rode on to the first of the cabins and called a halt to their short journey. The people spread out among the finished homes, setting up tents and shelters to house those who would wait for their own houses. There was no dispute among them, they just fell into a natural order of the first four wagons to pull in, got a house and the rest would wait. They too, were a good and generous people when not tyrannized by others. Thomas watched them settling in, then rode on to where work was progressing. He sought out his father. "Much has been accomplished," he commented from the back of his horse.

His father strode to stand beside him, a hand upon his leg. "Welcome home, Son." He pointed to the new people. "They are a weary lot."

"Aye, that they are, Father." He sighed. "As am I."

"Your vision was true, then? They were burned out and their numbers diminished?"

"Aye," Thomas answered, now dismounting to stand beside his father. He towered over the older man. "There's a story or two to be had when we've the time."

"Your mother awaits you at home. She and your sisters were sure today would be the time of your return." He smiled up at his only son. "I live with a household of visionaries, it seems."

"They were just hopeful, Father."

"Hopeful you were bringing home a new sister, I believe."

Thomas reddened in embarrassment. "No, Father. Not on this trip."

"Well, as I've said before, there's time for that. Right now, we have homes to build."

"And a church. I believe their pastor will want a

170

small chapel for their own."

Edward Woodslee nodded his head. "It will take some time for them to be comfortable within our own numbers, I suppose."

They walked among the new homes and the frames of others, planning the layout of the new little village. Father Jonathan joined them, as did Edward Stuart. It was decided that the new group would rest for a couple of days, then the building would begin again in earnest. The men who had been working on the new homes were delighted for the time to go home and be with their own families. "There's a small group behind us," Thomas explained. "But, their families are here. They should be along in only a day or two."

The group waited three days, then being rested and fed well, they began building their new village. Many hands make work go faster, so within twelve days they had nearly all the homes completed and were working on the chapel. Thomas laid out a plot of his own, about half way between the two communities. There, he planned to build his own blacksmith and iron works shop. He framed the shop, a barn, and a new house for himself with the help of a few friends.

"Are you expecting many sons?" His father asked with a twinkle in his eyes as he stopped by one evening.

"That's the shop, Father." Thomas pointed. "There is the house. It is much smaller."

"Smaller, yes," smiled his father, "but still..." He walked away before his son could comment.

* * * * * * * * * * * * *

Frederick Wilder and George Bays stood on the top of the escarpment, looking down at the lush valley. They could see the large community to their left and their own little village to their right, with the shining water of the inlet, greeting them. It was quite a contrast.

"There must be four or five hundred people down there," George indicated the larger community.

"The noise must be unbearable," commented Frederick. They watched for a moment longer. Then Frederick placed a hand on George's shoulder. "My Friend, let's go home." With that, they walked down the road, leading their horses behind them.

Thomas saw them first and ran to greet them. "Hail!" He called. "Welcome to your new home!"

They shook hands and clapped each other on the back as men are wont to do. Thomas walked them to the cabins their families had chosen and watched as they entered their abodes. He was anxious for the news, to know why they returned alone, but he knew they needed to be with their families first. He went to the little cabin behind the chapel. "Father, Frederick and George have arrived. They are with their families, but they are alone and I'm sure there will be stories to share."

"Alone?" He asked in concern. "I'll alert Brother

Stuart, then see the men and call for a meeting. Perhaps tomorrow, when they are rested."

"Aye," answered Thomas. Reluctantly, he went to his own property where he was still building his home. Father Jonathan walked with him, but turned off on a small track to the right which led to the home of Edward Stuart.

Edward had chosen to build his and Diana's house across the road from Thomas, and behind some boulders and trees. The house was closer to the eastern escarpment than the others, and more secluded. "We like our privacy," he explained. "We're used to being alone, away from the others."

The next morning, the men all met in the chapel. There were six men present, Thomas having invited his father in whom he had confided the stories he had been told. His father was a discerning man and Thomas knew he would use good judgement. Beside he and his father, there was Father Jonathan, Frederick Wilder, George Bays, and Edward Stuart, Diana Macklin's uncle.

"You mean to say, our little Rachel is alive?" Edward Stuart asked in astonishment. "That she, of all people, escaped Sarah's murderous ways? That little child withstood the evil?"

"Yes, but not without grievous injuries," replied George Bays.

"And this William person has taken up with my Diana?"

"He has, it seems, although Sister Macklin is

being, well, Diana."

Edward chuckled at that. "She hasn't remained unmarried without reason," he commented. "As wonderful as she is, she has not had any serious suitors, even though there was a time we all thought she would marry Will Armstrong."

Father Jonathan was thoughtful throughout the interview. All of these men had, it seemed, a story to tell. Each story seemed to fit a pattern that touched all their lives and brought everyone to this point. *Yet,* he reflected. *These stories were all going on around me as we lived together in the village, and I had no idea of them, or at least how they were formulating the culmination of all our lives. I must be blind or oblivious in the extreme! I had little hints and great fears, but I never acted upon any of them.* He looked around him at the men of his village. *These men asked questions then went in search of the answers. What a fool I am to think I lead them at all! They are the leaders. What is my job, then?*

"You say this man, what is his name?" Edward Woodslee asked.

"Will, William Avery," answered Frederick.

"You say he is a physician of extraordinary skill?"

"He is. He took Rachel's face and made it whole again. We didn't see it because the girl hid from us, but Sister Macklin told us of the miracle he performed."

"Yes, they should be only a few days behind

us." George answered. "They were going to try to persuade Rachel to come along, but she was reluctant. We built her a house out of the ruins of the old barn there at the Stuart place. She will be comfortable enough, and they are going to leave her a horse."

Father Jonathan now spoke up. "You mean to leave her there alone?" He asked in disbelief.

"I don't think she'll come with them. She's shy about her disfigured face." Frederick explained, while George nodded in agreement.

"And she may have other issues, as well," George said quietly. "Strange things have happened in the short life of that girl."

"But, she's no more than a child! How will she survive?" Father Jonathan persisted.

"She's survived up until now, just fine. She's built that little shelter. It wasn't much, but she would have made it through the winter in it, I think. She's canny, that one."

"And she's far from being a child now, Father." George said, a little shyly. "She's blossomed into a young woman."

"But, wouldn't she want to come and live with us?" Edward Stuart asked. "We're her only family, now. She's always loved Diana. Surely, she'll come."

"I don't think so," Frederick was shaking his head. "She's not a child anymore, like I said. She's been through tragedy and has survived." He paused and rubbed a hand over his beard. "The boys were right about one thing, she's girl and woman, but I think more woman somehow. William says her scars will heal in time and maybe then she'll want to see others. The only ones who've seen her now are Sister Macklin and William."

"How could I have let all of this happen?" Father Jonathan muttered, more to himself than to the roomful of men.

"How is it your fault?" Asked Thomas.

"I am supposed to be the one leading this people and now their lives are all in a shambles. This dear girl has been obviously tortured, surviving on her own..."

"I don't think they brought their troubles to you, Sir. You couldn't help what you didn't know about."

"No, they didn't, you're right. And I didn't seek them out, either. I ignored what I knew was wrong. I had my own doubts and fears, but I just couldn't believe in the evil I feared." He hung his head, shaking it in sorrow. He looked up again. "And then, after Marianne Armstrong was among us, it was easier to blame her for everything. And I did!" He closed his eyes, his great head shaking again. "I did!"

Edward Woodslee spoke, pulling gently at his bottom lip. "There are many mysteries in this old world, I think. For some reason we humans believe it is our duty to solve them or to be in control of them. But, in the grand scheme of things, we are truly only here to learn, do the best we can do with our knowledge for our fellow men, then die. Our knowledge and experiences are the only things we can take with us at that time, so aren't they really the only important things we possess? And each of us is ultimately accountable for the things we learn and the choices we make. We cannot take on the burdens of others, even our own children." He smiled and patted his son on the shoulder. "If we have been diligent in passing on our knowledge to the best of our ability, then we are really only accountable for our own selves."

"Thank you," Father Jonathan smiled. "I'll try to remember that, but I am the, or at least, I am supposed to be the spiritual leader of these people, and I don't think I've protected them very well, spiritually or otherwise."

"Be that as it may, we cannot change the past. We can only continue on from the moment we have new knowledge, understanding, and the change it brings about in one's heart. It is only the future which counts now."

"I am going to return for Diana and this new man, William." Announced Thomas, suddenly into the conversation.

His father sighed, and nodded sagely. "I know," he murmured.

They looked long into one another's eyes. Then Thomas continued. "I know my new home isn't completed yet, but I am compelled to return."

"For you," commented his father. "This is where the past, the present, and perhaps the future meet and meld into the eternities."

"I wish I'd said that," sighed Father Jonathan. "It is sage advise."

"But, beware of the fog if you are going back to the old village," advised Frederick Wilder. "We watched it behind us as we traveled. It was difficult to tell if it was enveloping the village or not."

"I don't think it was," George Bays interjected, wagging his head sagely. "It seemed to me to be behind the village quite a ways. But, as Frederick says, we aren't sure."

"Are Diana and Rachel in some kind of trouble, then?" Asked Diana's uncle. "Does this fog you speak of threaten them in some way?"

"No," Frederick answered. "They know about the fog and they seem to have some kind of communication with Sister Armstrong, if that's who it is."

"I think she might even protect them from the fog," commented George.

"I will leave at first light," Thomas said in an aside to his father. He rose, bid everyone a good night, and left the building.

"Yes," his father commented, staring after the retreating figure.

Soon after these events, the other men went to their homes for the remainder of the night. Thomas returned to the house of Father Jonathan. "Excuse me, Sir," he began, twirling his hat in his hands. "Would you tell me the history of the girl, Rachel Stuart?"

"Come in, come in, Lad!" Father Jonathan motioned him inside the small cottage. "Rachel, is it?" He asked, contemplating the past as he eyed the young man before him. They sat at the table in the center of the main room. "She was a delightful child, precocious, caring. Her parents had been so happy about her birth." A frown crossed his face. "I think Sarah Stuart, her grandmother, you know, was jealous. Not only of the child, but that her son had found such happiness in his life. Somehow, happiness eluded Sarah, or perhaps she scared it away." He pulled at his lower lip, lost in his reverie.

"And as a young woman?" Thomas prompted.

"What? Er, I suppose I don't really know. I keep thinking of her as a child. It's been about two years since I've actually seen her, I would guess." He rubbed at his mouth. "Let's see, her mother was the only child of the Smith's. They owned and operated the mill and granary. They were good, God-fearing people. Elijah, Rachel's father was a delightful young man. He was respectful of his elders and helpful to not only his father, but everyone in the village. He was handsome and gregarious, laughing often, to the distaste of his mother. Sarah seemed more in control of herself when Elijah was alive. Then, he fell in love with the beautiful Ruth Smith. Sarah did all she could to stop their union, but Elijah proved to have steel of his own in his veins. As I said, when Rachel was born, Elijah and Ruth were joyous. Then, they sickened and died, leaving Rachel to his mother.

Ruth's own parents died in a house fire shortly after. I don't know how Rachel has survived." His frown deepened, causing two furrows between his eyebrows. "We thought she was sick for such a long time, then that she too, had died. I tried to visit her a few times when Sarah first told us of her illness, but she wouldn't let me see her. There was always an excuse. Then Elias died from that fall and Rachel seemed to become even more ill, until she presumably died." His sigh filled the little room. "Sarah was such a formidable woman, daunting. Well, of course, those are only my own excuses." He lifted his hands in resignation.

"Thank you, Father. I leave early in the morning. Thank you, again." With that, Thomas strode to the door and was gone.

Father Jonathan sat for a long time, looking at the embers in his fireplace.

* * * * * * * * * * * * * *

Thomas rode out of the valley just as the sky was beginning to lighten. He rode hard for the first day so he could be into the valley beyond on the evening of the second day. He could take short cuts through the forest with his horse which hadn't been possible with wagons and carriages. Before turning off the road he looked through his glass to see any sign of travelers. There was no sign of Diana or the stranger, William along the trail. When he broke back out onto the roadway, he dismounted and checked for signs of recent travel. There was none.

In the early mornings a light fog pervaded the forest, but he felt it was not the deep, penetrating fog that he'd been warned about. He built no fires, eating dried food and bread from his saddlebags instead. He filled his canteen from streams along the way, stopping only once for his horse to graze. He slowed his pace as he crossed the firewood clearing, and soon came around the curve in the road onto the main street of the deserted village ruins. He could clearly see the barn, now a house, at the far end of town. Lights shone from the windows and the open door. He eased his horse slowly along the deserted road toward the comfort the beckoning lights offered.

* * * * * * * * * * * * * * *

Diana and Rachel walked and talked day after day. They talked of the good times, but not much about the bad. At times, Diana thought the girl was opening up and would travel with them when they were ready to leave. Then, for little or no apparent reason, Rachel ceased communication.

"She's trying to distance us, I think," Diana commented to William. "It's like she wants to trust us but something is holding her back, so she puts up walls to block us out."

"That's exactly what she _is_ doing," he agreed. "People with great burdens of grief, especially those who have been abused in some way, often react in just this way. They lose their trust in everyone, especially those they love the best. After all, someone she should have been able to count on for love and protection was her tormentor."

"But I've never done anything to hurt her!"

"I know that. And perhaps, even she knows that." He sighed. "But, to the tortured mind, no one came to rescue her, either. It is almost the same or worse than the abuse she suffered."

"Why, why didn't I see what was happening to her?" Diana wailed.

"You wouldn't have recognized the symptoms. She would have hidden anything wrong from you because of fear and shame and blame. The tormentor is very adept at putting the blame upon the shoulders of those he, or she, chooses as victims."

"She never asked for help."

"I know."

"She even admits that!"

"I'm sure she does. It is a classic case of extreme abuse."

"How can one person wield that kind of control over another? And why?"

"It gives them a sense of power and security."

"She was truly insane, wasn't she?"

"Probably. From what I understand of the situation, Rachel wasn't her only victim. She virtually held the entire community under her thumb. If someone stood up to her she found a way to eliminate them. I think she's been killing people off for a very long time. Maybe much longer than anyone realized. It could have started when she was a child or young adult with the killing of a cat or dog or even something so small as a bird. Once she got the sense of power over the life of another being she was hooked." They were silent for a moment, each lost 'in their own thoughts. Then William commented. "It's strange, you know. I never considered that serial killing has been going on for as long as there have been people. I'm beginning to understand now that some things we've been blaming on modern day pressures have really always existed." He looked thoughtfully at Diana. "Perhaps there are no new problems, only new ways to deal with them."

"Rachel never stood up to her, you know. I was much more defiant than that sweet girl." Diana commented on her thoughts.

"But, you weren't so closely related to her. She couldn't wield enough power to include you, like her husband, son, and granddaughter."

They had walked to the creek as they talked. Now, Diana turned to look back at the house. "What are we going to do about her?"

"I think you know the answer."

"No, William! Please don't make me leave her!"

He placed his hands on her shoulders, causing her to look up at him. He kissed her on the forehead. "Diana," he started. "Now that she has had your companionship for a few weeks, and as she sees the healing of her face over the next few months, she will not be content to be alone for long."

"You sound so convincing," she sighed as she laid her head upon his chest.

"I have only known you for a short time, Diana. Yet, I never want to be away from you for long, myself." He said into her hair.

She looked up and met his kiss with the commitment of her own feelings for him. "You'll have to help me be strong when we tell her," she said against his cheek.

He pushed her back to look again into her face in the fading light of evening. "You'll have the strength when you need it. That is your character."

She turned to look back up the road. "Is that a horse coming?"

He looked, too. "I believe it is. We've been too long here, they are coming to see us home."

They started walking back up the incline from the creek to the house. The horse had stopped in front of the house and a lone rider was dismounting.

"Hello!" William called to the stranger.

"Why, it's Thomas!" Diana said, coming forward.

"Diana!" Thomas walked to meet them as they hurried up to him. He turned to shake hands with the man by her side. "And this must be William."

"Hello, Thomas." William smiled. "Have you come to fetch us, then?"

"Well, let's just say I've come to see you on your way." He smiled in return.

"You look tired," Diana observed. "Come in

and sup with us, then we'll see to a place for you to sleep."

"I'll look after your horse," William offered. He smiled broadly. "I've always wanted to say that."

As William walked away, Thomas frowned at his back, then extended his frown to Diana, a question on his face.

She shook her head. "He's a strange man, Thomas, but a good one. There are many things we take for granted that he has never done. Tending to horses may be one of them."

"So he is truly from beyond the fog?" Thomas looked back at William, who was leading his horse to the corral.

"He is," Diana nodded. They approached the door of the house and went inside to the light. The table had already been set for three. Diana took down one more plate, cup and fork. "We have company for supper, Rachel," she said softly, turning her head toward the loft.

"I'm not hungry," came the muffled reply.

"Should I leave?" Thomas asked quietly.

Diana shook her head. "Rachel, it's impolite. Come down and I'll fix your hair. You don't have to enter in the conversation, but it is time for you to see others who might drop by. Brother," she looked at Thomas. "I've forgotten your..."

"Woodslee," he answered without waiting for her to finish.

"Yes," she nodded. "Brother Woodslee brings

news of our family, of Uncle Edward and Father Jonathan. Please come down."

"No!" Was the emphatic reply.

"It's all right, truly," Thomas said, seating himself at the table. "Give her time. I'll be here for awhile. I understand her reluctance. Frederick and George told us the story. It is an amazing tale."

"Is supper ready?" William asked as he came through the door.

Diana smiled. *This is how it will be,* she thought. *Our life together will be just like this night. Someone will drop in because William will make friends easily and we will sup together.* She thought of Rachel up in the loft. *And perhaps,* she blushed slightly at the thought, hoping the men thought it was only the heat of the cooking fire. *Perhaps there will be children.* She set the stew on the table, not looking at either of the men. They were talking about horses and the building, so thankfully, didn't seem to notice her particularly. *When did I stop thinking that I might have my own children?* She wondered. *I used to dream of the day I would become a mother.* Her attention was brought back by a comment by Thomas.

"Rachel doesn't understand that I already know her," Thomas was saying.

"How is that?" Diana asked as she sat down at her place.

"She was at the Armstrong's when I stopped to talk with Will a few years ago. She was a child then, and I wasn't much older. I don't think she noticed me as she went running down the hill to the village, her hair flying in the sunlight." They laughed at that.

"I don't remember meeting you, but I do remember Will, that is, Brother Armstrong, talking about you." She said. "Even in your youth, you impressed him quite a lot."

"I'm grateful he thought kindly of me. Between he and my father, I have grown in much knowledge."

"I wish I had met him," commented William. "But, I think, under the circumstances, it would have been impossible. I believe he might have been an ances..., well, a relative of mine."

Diana listened in quiet astonishment as the two men talked of the past and the future as though they were one. It was bewildering and a little frightening.

"It's possible," Thomas answered. "There is a certain family resemblance. How many generations, do you think?"

William stroked his chin as he thought. "Well, what's the year?"

"1694."

"Then, let's see, it would have to be four, no five, or even six generations, I believe." He paused. "That is, if this is truly the seventeenth century. Time here seems to be a relative thing. Or perhaps it is only relative for those who can cross the fog from one era to the other. I'm not sure how you folks got stuck in this era while the rest of the world seems to have gone on without you. It does connect with that deep fog."

"Crossing the fog seems to be what Mary, or Marianne does. I'm not sure how she manages to go from one world to the other. I'm not sure why some of us can see into the world beyond the fog from time to time, but I think," he pushed his food around on his plate. "I think that event might be over. There seems to be a change."

"Why is that?" William asked with interest. "I've wondered about it myself, but please tell me your ideas."

"I'm not totally sure. It's more a feeling than a fact." He frowned as he tried to formulate his ideas into words. "I think the past twenty years has been evolving to a particular conclusion. My father and I have spoken of it many times, trying to sort out all the facts and make some sense of it. In light of recent events, the uncontrollable fires, the advent of mysterious, disappearing women, the appearance of yourself," he indicated William with his fork. "We think it may all have started with some phenomenon of Rachel's parents, or at least her mother."

"Ruth?" Diana asked, joining in the conversation for the first time.

"If that was her name," nodded Thomas.

"Yes, Ruth Smith. But, how does she fit into the tale, exactly?" She asked.

"Perhaps she had a strong will to live, strong enough to keep her from passing on when she finally died at the hand of another." He paused. "Then, maybe Rachel kept her memory alive in her child's way. Now enters Mary, living with our people, but somehow watching Rachel grow. As long as Rachel's grandfather could protect her, Mary felt at peace. But, something happened. She felt she needed to be closer to her daughter. An opportunity arose, or she brought it about, and she became Marianne."

William gave a low whistle.

"It's conjecture, I know," said Thomas. "But...."

"So, Mary appeared around the time Ruth died, and Marianne appeared around the time of the plane crash, perhaps impersonating someone on the plane itself." William said in amazement. "Wow! That's deep."

Diana got up and walked to the loft ladder and looked up into the face of a very amazed Rachel at the top, peering down. She turned to face the men. "Then, Marianne tried to have as much influence on Rachel as possible within the role she'd taken on."

"Possibly."

"Do you think she knew? Or was the amnesia true? She seemed so sincere, yet so confused."

"I'm not sure we'll ever know the answers. Especially since we are not sure any of this is fact." Thomas answered.

"What happened in your world, William. How did you meet Marianne?" She asked. "We've never spoken of it."

"Well, I met her at the hospital, of course."

"The what?" Diana interrupted.

"Well, it's a building...never mind, Diana, I'll

explain that part later." He quickly gathered his thoughts again. "As a doctor, a physician, I treated her for burns, and other wounds. She resembled a girl from occupants of the airplane which crashed. That family tried to claim her, but there was something strange about her. She never really fit their family mold. I didn't think she was this Julie Kincaid, so she was released into the custody of one of our nurses when it was time for her to leave the hospital, because we could never really prove who she was. She, of course, insisted she was Marianne Armstrong." He frowned at the memories.

"We, that is Anita and I, uh, she was the nurse, decided to bring Marianne or Julie, whoever she was, out into the forest to see if her memory would return and we could help her. Now, I wonder if she planted that idea into our heads somehow." He smiled. "She led us on a merry chase for what seemed like days on end in the fog. Anita and I marked the trail and soon discovered we were going around in circles. We'd been nowhere at all. Marianne was enraged when she found out about the markers. She said it tied us to our world. We decided then, that she was insane and we needed to get help. We were in way too deep. I was in no shape to do anything with my pneumonia, so Anita went back and Marianne brought me through the fog, here." He pointed to the table in front of him.

"And now?" Thomas asked. "Is she still here?"

"Only sometimes," Diana replied. "I've seen her

in the distance, but not for several days. Have you seen her, William?"

"No, not since we first came down here to the village." He shook his head.

"I have," Rachel offered from the top of the ladder.

Diana smiled up at her. "Will you come down now? We're all friends. You know Thomas, don't you?"

Rachel nodded. "I'm not ready."

William spoke up. " I think this Kincaid family is probably related to, uh, what did you say Rachel's mother's name was?" He directed to Diana.

"Ruth. Ruth Smith."

"Yes, well, that would explain the resemblance and the feelings of the family."

"And it neatly ties this all together, doesn't it?" Thomas added.

"Yes. Yes, it does," Diana said. "It is unimaginable, but I'm beginning to believe it is all true."

William smiled at her. "On that note; Thomas, you look exhausted. Let me show you the neat little cottage Rachel built for us to stay in so the women can have this nice, comfortable house."

"A full stomach and sleep," Thomas said, patting his abdomen. "I couldn't ask for more tonight."

They said their good nights while Diana cleaned up the dishes and put the fire out. She felt rather than heard Rachel join her. "Diana," Rachel urged. "If all of this is true, then Marianne really was my mother, wasn't she?" She was on the verge of tears.

"I don't know, Rachel," Diana answered truthfully. "But, it certainly seems like it."

Rachel nodded in the dim light from a single lamp. She started back to the loft ladder, then turned to face Diana who was looking after her. "Am I keeping her here?"

"Do you think you might be?"

Rachel thought for a moment. Then, she nodded. "Yes," she said. "From the time I was little, back to my earliest memories, I have pled with her to be with me, to never leave me with..." she sighed deeply.

"Ruth was so excited when you were born," Diana said. "She held you all the time." Diana smiled sadly. "That is, when Elijah would let her. He held you the rest of the time. Oh, Rachel, they loved you so much!" She moved to hold the now crying girl in her arms. "They still do. They always will, even from the other side."

"I know," Rachel whispered. "I know."

They slept on Diana's bed, wrapped tightly in one another's arms, neither willing to let the other go. Diana felt the release of the burdens Rachel carried as she cried herself to sleep. *At last,* she thought. *At last, perhaps Rachel is going to heal. Thank God for Thomas and William! Now, we'll be able to go home.* With that, she fell into a deep sleep.

In the morning, Rachel was nowhere to be found. Diana was frantic, calling, and hunting for the girl. Thomas and William looked for awhile, too. But, finally, Thomas called a halt to the search. "Let's wait," he said. "She heard all we had to say. She needs time to come to grips with it all."

"I agree," stated William.

Diana looked from one to the other of the men. They were right, and she knew it. *I still want to protect her as though she were a child,* she admitted to herself. *Even Rachel is more mature than I am.* "You're right," she acknowledged. "I know you're right, but I still feel torn by it."

"You are a natural mother," William smiled at her. "That is a very good sign."

Thomas raised his eyebrows as Diana blushed furiously. "I have things to do," she mumbled as she turned and strode toward the relative safety of the house.

Thomas watched her walk away, then turned his attention to William, who was still smiling, also watching Diana. "It's as Frederick said," he commented.

William looked up at him. "What did Ole Fred say?" He asked in amusement.

"I take it that means Frederick," Thomas said hesitantly.

"Yes," William laughed at the confused look on Thomas' face.

"He said there were feelings between you and Diana," he nodded toward the house.

"I hope that's true," William said as he laid a friendly hand on Thomas' shoulder. "My Friend, I hope that is the truth."

When Rachel hadn't returned by late afternoon, Thomas saddled his horse to ride after her. He started up the hill to Diana's old home, but as soon as he topped the ridge, he knew it was the wrong choice. He knew instantly where she would be. He turned his horse along the rutted roadway to the old Armstrong cabin. The sun was bright and hot, but as he neared the home site, he could see fog rising out of the river valley. He slowed his horse to a walk as he came within sight of the barn and back of the house. When he reached the fence, he dismounted and tied his horse to the garden gate. He stepped softly along the side of the cabin to the front porch and sat with his back against the wall of the cabin. He didn't say a word, nor did he look at Rachel sitting on the far side of the porch from him, he just looked out over the river valley where the fog was rising despite the hot afternoon sun. Time drew on and occasional flies buzzed around them.

"I knew you would come." She finally whispered into the sunshine.

Thomas nodded in answer. "Have you been with her?" He asked, indicating the fog before them.

"No," she shook her head. "Unless she is coming with that fog bank, I fear she's gone forever."

"Except in your memory," he said kindly.

They sat quietly then, watching the fog as it lifted and fell with the breeze generated by the rushing of the water far below. The mysterious fog never came to the top of the hill, but wafted in the moisture of the valley. Afternoon became evening, and Thomas rose to turn his horse into the field where it would have access to grass and water. When he returned, she had not moved. Evening became night and still, they sat watching, waiting. They had no need to talk and break the spell of the air around them. Thomas could feel her pain and apprehension, and Rachel could feel his support and respect. It was enough for them both.

* * * * * * * * * * * * * *

Hand in hand, Diana and William walked along the roadway through the burned-out village as they waited for Rachel and Thomas to return. "Do you think he found her?" Diana asked with worry in her voice.

"Yes," he said.

"How can you be so positive about everything?" She asked. She couldn't keep the exasperation from her voice. "You are always so confidant."

"I'm glad I fool someone," he teased, smiling at her. "I am so confused about my new role in life; enough even for you, I think.

They walked on in silence for a few moments. "She'll come home with us, now." Diana said with a long sigh.

"You're wrong, Diana. Quit pinning your hopes on that. She won't come."

"But, she and I made a huge breakthrough! I'm sure she'll be willing to come home, now!"

"She won't, I tell you. She isn't ready. She may never be ready for that. It's probably one of the biggest reasons she disappeared today. She can't think or act without hurting you."

Diana drew away from him. "Surely you are wrong!" She stated hotly. "She's family! These are all people she knows! She will come home! She will!" Diana couldn't fight the tears which spilled in profusion down her cheeks.

William took her gently by the shoulders. "Diana, I know how much you want to mother this girl, but she has got to have the space to be her own person. She is not a child, but a woman, grown. That's why she's gone now. She needs to work this out in her own way. You cannot do it for her. You can be her friend, her cousin, even. But, you cannot take away the hurts and you can't force her to do what you think is the right thing." He paused, looking lovingly into her eyes. "Even if it is the right thing."

Diana looked away from him, but sighed in resignation, her shoulders sagging noticably.

"I know how much you love her, and she loves you. But, she has to work out her life in her own way. And that will probably mean she will stay here, at least for now."

"I can't leave her alone, William. I can't!" Her eyes sought out his, beseechingly. "Please, understand."

"I do understand." He looked at her for a moment,

searching her face, then leaned forward and kissed her, long and fervently. She melded into him as though she were a part of his own body.

There they stood in one another's arms when they heard the soft footfalls of a horse coming out of the gloom of the forest, east of town. Diana tensed in anticipation, turning to see. They watched in silence until they could both see, not a horse, but a mule carrying Father Jonathan.

"Hello! Hello!" He called as he came abreast of the couple. He pulled his mule to a halt with some effort. "Well," he smiled. "It looks as though I've arrived just in time."

"Is the whole community coming back?" Diana asked.

"No, no!" Father Jonathan laughed after he had successfully dismounted. "I just felt compelled to follow that young man after we heard all that had happened here."

"Come in the house and eat," Diana suggested. "We have some soup and a little bread."

"I'll see to your mule," volunteered William. "That seems to be my job around here."

"You must be, uh, Brother Avery, is that correct?" Father Jonathan offered his hand.

"William, just call me William or Will." He shook his head, with a tired smile.

"We try to keep some decorum in the village, Brother Avery," the monk said, then turned to Diana. "More than food," he said. "I hope you have a bed.

I am sore, tired!"

"Father," said Diana. "Don't you think the formal names were just part of Sarah's control over everyone? Perhaps if we are friendlier with one another we will avert another disaster."

"Tch-tch-tch," he muttered. "I don't know, Sister Macklin. We'll see, we'll see."

They ate together, quietly discussing the events of the past few days. "So, she ran away, then?" Father Jonathan queried.

"Not really, Father," William said respectfully. "I believe Thomas will return with her soon, tonight or tomorrow."

"He and his father are good men, as are most others in our new area. They have built homes for us in a matter of weeks and subscribed fields for us to plant and call our own. It is true charity of a kind not seen before by our people. We are all truly overwhelmed, and so very grateful."

"Is Uncle Edward comfortable, then?" Diana asked.

The monk laughed. "He'll be so angry when he finds I've come on this journey and left him behind!"

"Why did you come?" William asked.

"I'm not sure," he replied. "But, I couldn't eat or sleep without the thought being there that I needed to be here. So, here I am!" He smiled broadly at the couple sitting across the table from him.

They talked awhile longer, then William made

another bed in the small room built by Rachel. "I'd give you Thomas' bed, but he may return in the night."

Darkness settled on the village and the hills surrounding it. Sleep didn't come easily for those waiting for the morning light.

* * * * * * * * * * * * * *

At the cabin on the hill, Thomas napped off and on against his knees. Rachel seemed not to sleep at all, but sat watching the approaching fog. The moon cast it's silvery light upon the cabin and surrounding hillside. Thomas looked up at Rachel as the moonlight touched her face. He could only see the left side of her face, and what he saw made his breath catch in his chest. She was a lovely young woman. Her features were fine and flawless. Her black hair was thick and wavy in the night. Thomas smiled to himself and closed his eyes as he laid his head against his knees once again. The night wore on. In the first, gray light of predawn, the fog reached it's tentacles across the hill toward the cabin. At last, Rachel rose and walked to the edge of the fog. She stood waiting and was soon rewarded by the vision of her mother, walking from within the fog to greet her. "Mother," Rachel breathed.

"Hello, Rachel." She smiled at the girl. Her thick, black hair blew with a breeze Rachel couldn't feel. Nor was there any dampness in this eerie fog. It simply existed.

"So, you <u>are</u> my mother," Rachel said simply.

"Yes." She nodded. "You have finally seen me as I am."

"Have I caused you to appear?"

"Yes."

"You're not Marianne." It was a statement, not a question.

"I'm not, now. You have knowledge now of me as I am."

"Why, when I asked you before, didn't you tell me you were my mother?"

"I didn't understand at that time who I really was and you nor others were ready to receive the knowledge to let me be me. I knew the changes had to do with you, but I was confused, as well. Now, we have both grown in knowledge and love."

"So, now you and I both know? That's what makes this difference?"

"Yes." She nodded, with a kind smile.

"You look like me," Rachel said shyly.

Ruth smiled. "I believe, My Dear, that you look like me."

Rachel's hand went to her face. "Not any more." She whispered sadly.

"That will change with time, Rachel. You'll see that love and time will help you."

"Have I been keeping you from..." Rachel looked up with pleading in her eyes.

"It was a mission I had to fulfill. Now, you are safe."

"So, you'll leave me?" Fear welled up within Rachel's breast and she cried out. "Mother, please don't leave me! I've only just found you, don't leave me now!"

"You have Thomas, and Diana, and William. There are many who love you."

Rachel nodded, tears flooding her cheeks. She put a hand up to her right eye. It came away wet. "My eye tears again," she observed.

"Yes, you will heal much, yet, Dear Rachel." She stepped forward and took the now sobbing girl in her arms.

"You're real! I can feel you, you <u>are</u> real!"

"Yes, I have always been real, Rachel." She stroked the girl's face and head. "But, I am no longer a true part of the world as you know it. My mission to see you to safety, is over. Now, your life may begin."

Rachel clung to her mother in the mists of the fog, but the sun was rising and the fog was becoming thin. "I love you, Rachel. Always remember that I love you." Her mother pushed the girl to stand back facing her, then she looked beyond Rachel's shoulder and smiled.

Thomas reached out to place his hands on Rachel's shoulders as her mother's hands slid away. He nodded to her as he pulled Rachel closer to him, and she nodded slightly in return, just before the fog and her image faded in the brightness of the morning sun. Rachel felt his hands upon her, yet stood watching as her mother faded from view. The river was suddenly

201

in front of them, down the hill in its winding valley. It shone like a ribbon in the fresh morning air. The air was clear and warm.

"It's time," he whispered into her hair.

She nodded slightly, but stood as though rooted to the spot. Thomas left her side and brought his horse to where she remained. He mounted, then reached down and put his hand upon her arm. Without looking up at him, she placed a foot in the stirrup of his saddle and swung effortlessly up behind him. As they rode slowly down the road, she rested her head on his back. They approached the ravine where her grandmother lay buried and she asked him to stop. After he tied the horse to a tree, he climbed down into the ravine with her. "I'm sorry, Grandmother," she sobbed, falling to her knees upon the dirt of the grave.

"Rachel," Thomas pulled her up to rest against his chest. "This is not your fault. The woman was insane and she hurt you in her pain. Her death, at her own hand, was a release from that pain. She used you to do what she was too cowardly to do alone. But, you did not do anything wrong. In the end, it was all about herself."

"Thank you," she whispered as she gained control of her crying.

"Let's find a stone and mark her grave, shall we?" He asked.

They spent some time rolling a large, smooth river stone onto the unmarked grave. They stood, Thomas with his hat in his hands, for a few moments. "I'm ready, now, Thomas," she finally breathed and turned abruptly to climb back up to the road. Thomas replaced his hat and followed her to the horse. They mounted, Thomas first, then he pulled Rachel up behind him. They rode silently to the burned out village and the house made from a barn.

Diana heard the horse first and jumped up from the table where she was eating breakfast with William and Father Jonathan. She ran to stand beside the horse before they were even stopped, and Rachel slid from the saddle into Diana's waiting arms. They stood there, crying together. Thomas dismounted, automatically handing the reins of his horse to the uplifted hands of William, who smiled mischievously at him. "That's me, the stable hand!" He said light-heartedly.

Thomas shook his head slightly as he tried to come to grips with William's levity. He looked at the monk with a question in his eyes. "You're here?"

Father Jonathan smiled, and clapped his hands softly together. "Yes! Yes, here I am, following your lead." He turned to look at the two women. "It really is our Rachel," he whispered.

Thomas turned slightly where he could see the women, as well. "It is, indeed," he answered. His face was in need of a shave and his eyes showed his exhaustion from the lack of a good night's sleep. But he could not keep the smile from his lips.

Rachel looked up from her place against Diana's

shoulder, then raised her head to look more closely with her good eye, at Thomas who was watching her. He smiled rather shyly, and Rachel returned it in kind. Then, she pushed herself away from Diana and walked to him, where she laid her head on his chest, just below his chin. "Thank you," she whispered.

Thomas put his arms around her awkwardly, then spoke into her hair. "You're welcome. Thank you."

Diana watched with mixed emotions as Rachel glided into the circle of Thomas' arms.

She didn't notice the shyness and awkwardness of their coming together. She felt a pang of jealously and resentment. *What are you thinking?* She berated herself. *Did you think Rachel would be yours and yours alone? Did you even hope she would just grow up in your own home, never tasting love and devotion to another? What foolish webs we weave for ourselves! Look at them. No wonder this young man came. His destiny has been shaped by this event as has my own.* She smiled at William as he joined them.

The three adults walked back into the house to their breakfast. Diana set two more plates on the table, but Rachel and Thomas weren't hungry. Rachel climbed to her loft after a quick hug for Diana. Thomas sought out his bed in the small room next to the root cellar.

It was a long day for Diana, but she, William, and Father Jonathan walked around the old village talking about the recent events, about the history of the village, and somewhat about the future. "I would like to go home soon," Diana said. "I'm sure Uncle Edward is anxious about me, and I am ready to begin a new life." She smiled sweetly at William.

"We could go tomorrow," he replied, winking at the monk. "The good Father is here to see us on our way."

"It would be my pleasure," he answered. "But, first I believe I will need to perform one little ordinance for the young couple we leave behind."

"What do you mean, Father?" Diana asked, frowning at William's all-knowing smile.

"A wedding, of course."

"No!"

"And why not?" William challenged.

"Why they're..." She looked away, toward the buildings where the two young people still slept the day away.

"Not children," he prompted, stepping up to encircle her in his arms.

"Oh, you!" She pushed at him playfully. "Do you really think so, Father?" She half turned to look at the monk.

"I cannot leave them here, alone, and unwed!" He said in mock horror.

"So," Diana mused. "All the shadows, and the fog, and the darkness will be left behind. Rachel will come out into the light of life, safe on the arm of a new husband." She nodded at her own analysis. "Yes, William," she added. "I am ready to go home now."

"Into the light of life," repeated Father Jonathan. "That is a prophecy for us all, a new life, a new village. Into the light of life."

Eight

New Brighton, At Last

There was no more talking that day. When Rachel and Thomas awoke, they wouldn't hear of any discussion with the others, but walked off into the woods to talk by themselves. As they sat in Rachel's favorite clearing, she poured out all the joys she had felt in this spot as a child. "I would hide here from all the sorrow and, well I guess it was evil, in our home. Grandfather didn't always have time to help me or to spend time with me, so I came here and pretended I was with my mother." She shook her head as tears ran down her face. She kept most of her face hidden with her hair now, so Thomas could only see a part of her face from where he stood. "I hid some treasures in the hole in the bottom of this tree," she said as she knelt to peer into the hole. "All my keepsakes burned up with the tree." She looked to the burned-out top of the old tree. Her hair fell back and Thomas could clearly see the scars that disfigured the right side of her head. They were still vibrant, mute evidence of the torture she had endured. Although not as bad to look at as Rachel, herself felt, the scarring was still angry in its coloration. There was the green-yellow of healing bruises around her eye and ear, evidence of the healing work of her surgery. William had explained to Thomas that Rachel would always bear the scars, but that time would soften the impact of their looks, they would become less noticeable and the color would become dull and not draw so much attention to her. She was fortunate to have thick hair so that it could be brushed across her head to cover the right side where the hair would no longer grow properly through the scar tissue just over and around her ear. The damage was only about a palm's span in size, but because it also spread to the front of her face, seemed much larger. As time worked its healing wonders, the actual injury would become less and less noticeable altogether. Watching her, Thomas was suddenly glad he hadn't seen her when she was more disfigured. He would never have that memory and she would know it. She would feel more confidant because she looked better when she met him.

On impulse, Thomas walked up behind Rachel and laid his right hand alongside her right cheek. She stiffened, but didn't draw away. "Can you accept me like this?" She whispered.

"Yes," he nodded. "Because I know that inside, you are really like this." He placed his left hand upon her left cheek. Her tears flowed over his hands and onto her own as she placed her hands upon his. He knelt down beside her and slipped his hands to her shoulders, causing her to turn toward him. She automatically swung her hair over her face, but he brushed it away. "Don't hide from me, Rachel," he bade of her. Shyly, she looked at him with her head tilted to the right as she had been training herself to do. Thomas bent down and quickly kissed her on the cheek. Rachel blushed furiously and looked at the ground, but she couldn't help the smile that stole first to her lips then to her entire countenance. She glanced up at him and he could see the joy infused on her face before the pain clouded her eyes once again. He nodded. "What do we do now, Rachel?" He asked. "For I'm not willing to leave you."

"And I'm not willing to go, yet."

"I know. You still cling to her, even though she made her plea of good-bye."

"I'm afraid. I love Diana, but I'm afraid to be without Mother, now." She bowed her head in her shame and sorrow. "I don't want to disappoint Diana. She has always been so good to me, so much like another mother."

"I believe she understands what you're going through. William certainly does. He will be a great comfort to her."

"I hope you're right. I just can't leave now. I can't."

"Then, if you are willing, I will stay here with you for a time. I can stay in the cabin you built or one of those up on the hill if it will make you feel more comfortable, but when I go, I want you to go with me. Can you do that?" He peered under her hair which had fallen across her lowered face.

"Why do you want to do that?" She asked in her girlish innocence.

"I'm not sure what love is," he began. "But, I think you and I were meant to be together and I find you not only lovely, but by your shyness, a complement to my own boldness. Does that make sense?"

She nodded, but pulled deeper into her hair as a turtle would into its shell. She could feel the telltale heat of her embarrassment creeping up her neck and infusing her face.

"The question is, am I acceptable to you?" He pushed at her hair and stuck it behind her left ear.

She immediately shook her hair down, but lifted her head and looked directly at Thomas. She still kept her face turned slightly to the right, but he could see both of her eyes. "I don't know what to say, Thomas." She said. "It sounds like a beautiful ending to a very sad story, but how can we know we will be happy if we should begin a life together? I have..." She couldn't finish, but looked away to the ground.

"No one can ever know the answer to that, Rachel. But, my parents are happy and I believe I can offer the kind of lasting happiness they know to you, if you will work with me to accomplishment it."

"I can't make this kind of decision, Thomas," she shook her head. "It is a thing, so big!" She raised her arms to indicate an enormous task. "And I feel so small." Her arms came down and she made a cup of her hands to indicate the difference. Her eyes portrayed the sadness she felt.

"The others need to go on with their lives," he said gently. "They cannot wait for you and I."

"I know," she said, rubbing her hands together. "Will they go if we say you're staying with me? Diana doesn't want to leave me here alone, I know."

"I believe they will go," he answered.

She nodded, then looked away. "I just wanted to be alone. I still feel like that." A great sigh escaped her. "It's not about you, Thomas, it's about me. I still feel like a little girl, but I'm always faced with big, adult decisions." Tears again washed over her face. She wiped at them, but it didn't help. "I just want to be me for awhile. I don't want to make any more decisions, or even to think. I just want to be."

Thomas pulled her to him and she didn't resist, but sobbed against his chest. He held her like that until her crying was spent, stroking her hair and her arm, alternately.

"If you will trust me, I will make these decisions. You will have your life, your privacy, your time to grow and heal. Then, we will talk of future things again. Agreed?"

She nodded, but didn't move from his embrace. They sat awhile longer, then rose and walked slowly back to the house. The last rays of the setting sun were touching the valley as they came into the house where the others were eating their evening meal. They joined in the meal, then Thomas began a conversation.

"I know you are all anxious to go to your new homes and get on with your lives," he began. "Please feel free to do that. Rachel and I will stay here. I will live in one of the homes untouched by the fires, up on the hills. She will stay here." He indicated the house they were in. "I will make sure she is not wanting for food or firewood or any other thing she might need. When the time comes, we will join you."

He looked pointedly at Rachel as silence spread over the group. No one knew what to say. Rachel glanced at Thomas, but made no effort to speak.

"Rachel," began Diana.

Rachel began shaking her head. "No, Diana," she said. "I'm not ready to go with you. I won't go."

"May I ask why?"

Rachel looked up. "I'm not ready to give up my mother," she said in her quiet whisper.

"Do you think she'll come back here?"

"Diana," Thomas interrupted. "Rachel has to work this out. She's the only one who can release the energy related to her mother. You can't help her."

Diana didn't fight the tears streaming down her face, but she refrained from saying any more. She got up from the table and hugged Rachel, then began cleaning up the dishes.

Rachel's tears were flowing again, as well. She accepted Diana's hug, then watched her as she worked. She made no move to rise or say anything to anyone.

Father Jonathan spoke up. "In light of this new

development, I have been thinking. I thought when I came here that I had come to perform a wedding or healing of some kind. Once again, I see that you have chosen the better way. But, if you will allow me, I would like to stay here with you children, for a time. I need to come to peace with my own ghosts who live here in this village. Not physical ghosts, of course, but memories of things I did and things I didn't do. Can you accept me here on those terms?" He looked around the group.

Thomas was nodding. "You can stay with me, if you like. I believe the Macklin home is the most comfortable right now. Is that all right with you, Diana?"

She turned to face them from her work. Wiping at her eyes, she nodded. "Yes, of course." She said, having to clear her throat to be heard. "That will bring everyone great peace, I think." She smiled slyly. "Except Uncle Edward."

"It isn't as I'd envisioned it, but this sounds like a good plan." William added to the conversation. He looked at Diana. "Shall we leave in the morning?"

She nodded. "The sooner, the better, I think," she said. "I'll not want to be going if we procrastinate much longer." She glanced at Rachel, who was looking back at her. "I don't want to leave now, but I see the wisdom of this plan."

Soon after supper, they retired to their respective beds. Diana thought Rachel might want to talk to her in the night, but before she knew what was happening, morning light filled the room through her window. She rose quietly and dressed, then washed her face and brushed her hair, before stepping outside. It didn't surprise her to see William hitching their horse to the little cart. His bag was sitting in the cart box. "Good morning," she greeted.

He smiled. "Good morning, yourself. Are you ready?"

"Aren't we going to say good-bye to anyone?"

"Let's leave them sleeping," he suggested, then pointed to a burlap bag sitting next to the cart. "I gathered some food stuffs. See if we have what we need, will you?"

She looked into the bag. It was sorely lacking. "I'll fill it up," she said. "These things can't be left to a man." She then disappeared into the house to retrieve her personal things and the items they would need on the trail.

William looked after her. *Did women's lib start back in the seventeenth century?* He wondered. *Differences between men and women and the way they think must be evident in every age of time.* He shook his head and went back to his work.

Diana started some water boiling on the stove and prepared to make mush for breakfast. While the water was heating, she carried her items out to the cart and put them into the box. Thomas and Father Jonathan were up and talking quietly with William. She didn't bother them, but went back into the house. Rachel was standing at the stove, staring into the pot of heating water.

"Good morning, Rachel," Diana gave her a quick hug.

She smiled and hugged back. "Good morning."

"Are you all right?"

"Yes," she said. "I was just thinking about how we use a stove for so many good things and how it can be misused." She absently ran a hand over her scarred face.

"Rachel, you'll never forget these things, I suppose." Diana said. "But, try not to dwell on them."

"I know," Rachel said, turning away from the stove, trying to smile bravely. "Are you ready to go?"

"Nearly," Diana looked out the open door. "We'll eat, then..." she trailed off into silence.

"It's really going to be fine, Diana," Rachel said. "I want you to go. I want to be alone. At least for a time, I want to be alone."

"Yes..." mused Diana.

"I still need to be a little girl, and I need to be a young woman. On my own, I need to feel the differences without the fear of disappointing someone else. It's for me, Diana. It's for me."

After a long, tear-choked embrace, they worked together to set the meal on the table before Diana went to the door. "We can eat, now," she said into the clear, morning air. The men walked into the house and sat at the table.

"It should only take you two or three days," Thomas said when they were finished with their meal. "The road is traveled now and the cart should have no troubles."

"Uncle Edward will be glad," Diana said.

"Apologize for me, will you?" Father Jonathan asked. "I know he must be upset with me for leaving him behind. But, he'll be happy once you are with him."

"I hope he'll be equally happy with me," William said.

"Father!" Diana exclaimed, suddenly alarmed. "You won't be there to..." she looked at William, then back at the monk. "I mean, well..." She looked back at William in some confusion.

William smiled as he took her hand. "I think she's wondering who will marry us, Father," he drawled.

Diana blushed. "Well..."

"But, in truth, I haven't asked her in so many words. We've talked of it, but I haven't said, 'Diana, will you marry me', yet." He looked at her with an ever widening smile. "Have I?"

She sighed in exasperation and looked at the ceiling, but did not withdraw her hand from his. "No," she said sardonically.

He laughed merrily and the others couldn't help but laugh with him. "Will you?" He finally said as the laughter died away. "Sister Macklin, will you marry me?"

She looked at him, barely able to keep from

smiling. Then, she closed her eyes and shook her head. "What am I getting into?" She muttered. Opening her eyes, she met his loving gaze with one of her own. "Yes, since that sounded so much like a proposal of marriage, I accept," she said.

"Then," he smiled at them all. "If the good Father will perform that ceremony here, we can honeymoon our way to Uncle Edward."

"Honeymoon?" She asked with raised eyebrows.

William threw up his hands. "I give up!" He said. "You are a most primitive people." He turned his attention to the smiling monk. "Father, will you marry us today so we can leave together?"

"I will!" He announced. "I don't know if Edward will ever forgive me, but I will, indeed!"

"Thomas, you get to be the best man, and I guess Rachel will be your maid of honor, so we're all set." William looked around the room at the astonished faces. "What?" He frowned, sitting back in his chair and looking from one to another of them.

Diana began to laugh, then Rachel snickered into her hand.

William shook his head. "Oh, never mind!" He said. "Father, shall we get this over with?"

They moved outside where Father Jonathan performed the simple ceremony that united Diana and William, with Rachel and Thomas as witnesses. They all hugged and shook hands and cried, then the happy couple climbed aboard their cart and drove away. As they neared the curve into the forest, Diana turned and waved. Rachel and Thomas waved in return, then they disappeared from view. Diana sighed as she turned back to face her future.

"They'll be fine," William said.

"I know," she answered. "But, will we?"

"What do you mean?" He asked, frowning.

"Just that you have so much to learn," she said, smiling sweetly as she slipped her arm into his.

It took him a moment to recover from her teasing. "My Dear," he said. "We will also be just fine, just fine, indeed!" With that, he urged their horse forward at a faster pace.

They took four, blissful days to reach the top of the escarpment where the road turned to begin its descent. The days were warm and fragrant with the smell of pines. The nights were equally blissful. They shared all their hopes and dreams. They shared stories of family, childhood, and William entertained Diana with stories of his high school days. She couldn't imagine what it had been like to drive a car or go to the movies.

At last, they stood together, looking at the vista laying in the bright sunlight. "Look at that!" Diana said with a sweep of her arm. "Isn't is beautiful?"

"This must be the new village," William pointed to their right. "And look at the water. It would be nice to have a good swim."

"You'll have to teach me," she said, laying her head on his shoulder.

218

He slipped his arms around her, then swept her up into them, swinging her around to face the cart. "You've never been swimming?"

"No," she laughed as he set her down. "Mother would never allow more than wading, and not even that sometimes. But, I used to watch others and feel envious of their fun." She frowned momentarily. "Then I'd always feel guilty, of course, for the envy."

He laughed. "Well, I suppose I will be a black sheep among your people, then." He said. "For I will teach all of our children to swim and to hunt and to do everything!"

"All of them?" Diana laughed.

"Yes, all of them; however many that is!"

Happily, Diana climbed into the cart as William began leading the horse down the steep path to the bottom of the cliff wall. They moved slowly to where the main road cut through the middle of the valley. "Which way?" He asked.

"I'm not sure," she answered. "I think Father said to go to the left toward the town, there." She pointed.

He came back and sat with her in the cart, then drove onto the main road. They passed the new chapel and Diana said. "It's the first road to the right after the chapel, isn't that what he said?"

"I believe you're right," William answered. He pulled the reins and the horse turned neatly into the track toward the eastern escarpment. As they rounded a small copse of trees and a jungle of large boulders, the new house and barn were suddenly before them.

"Oh, my!" Diana breathed. "Can this truly be our home?"

"It's bigger than the old one," William observed.

"Yes. Yes, it is!" Excitement was filling her as the horse came to a halt at the hitching rail in front of the small barn. Diana jumped off the cart, leaving William to tie up the horse.

"I knew you would come today!" Uncle Edward called as he half ran from the open barn door. They met in a warm and teary embrace. Then, Edward pointed over Diana's shoulder. "And this? Is this my new nephew, William?"

"Yes!" Diana turned, slipping an arm around her uncle. "Will, come and meet your Uncle Edward."

William walked forward, hand outstretched. "It's nice to meet you, Sir."

"He's polite!" Edward observed. "I like him already."

"May I ask, Sir, why you call me your nephew? Is there a, uh, messenger who came before us?"

Edward laughed. "No, no, Lad!" He said. "But, my old friend, the Father, left to come after you and I know he wouldn't let you come on along without him if it weren't proper to do so." He smiled at his niece. "And, I know Diana better than anyone. That glow about her is not from a weary trail. No, I knew it the moment I saw her happy face." He peered at William keenly. "And, a man has a protective way about him when he has a wife to care for." He stepped up to the cart and grabbed a sack. "Come, let's get your things settled in the house. And this horse needs tended to, as well." He wiped at his eyes with his shirt sleeve as he walked away from the couple. "The house is in desperate need of a woman's touch, I'm afraid."

"I guess I'll tend to the horse, of course," William smiled at Diana.

She reached up and kissed him lightly on the cheek. "I can hardly wait to explore the village and the fields, oh, the entire valley!" She bubbled. "But, I think I'll start with the new house, first."

William smiled after her as she carried her bags into the house. He led the horse into the barn where he unhitched the cart, then led the animal into a stall and rubbed it down with dry hay. He gave the horse water and a little grain from a bucket, then turned him loose into a small field. He watched as the horse ran and kicked, then dropped to the ground to roll. *And now, what will you do, William Avery?* He asked himself. *Like this horse, you are free of all the fetters of your former existence. Now, you can run and jump and roll into a new, rather old, life. You have a wife and a responsibility to a people you know virtually nothing about.* He picked up a piece of straw to chew on and leaned against the door of the barn. *Can I truly be a physician to these people? I have only little equipment, and no medicines. Of course, my wife is a 'healer' of some renown and can teach me about herbs and their uses. I know some chemistry, perhaps I can develop some remedies with her help.* The horse whinnied into the air and another answered from some distance away. He smiled ruefully. *Perhaps I'll become a farmer. I keep getting stuck with the horses. I wonder who did this before I came along.* He shook his head slightly. *Face it, Will, old boy, you're afraid of this 'new' future. You're used to modern luxuries and this primitive society doesn't fit the bill. Yet, remember how as a boy, you always wanted to be one of the pioneers? You were always sure you had been born into the wrong generation. Here's your chance. The impossible has happened and you...* He shook his head again, threw down the straw, and turned to leave the barn. *You've just got to live. It does no good to think of...* Diana was watching him from the barn door. He smiled as he saw her. *This is real!* He thought as he reached her and swept her up into his arms. He swung her around and put her back on the ground before kissing her.

Diana laughed aloud. "I was going to ask you what you were thinking, but I don't think I really want to know."

"Just about the changes life takes, that's all," he said.

"Uncle Edward has some venison and potatoes cooked. Are you hungry?"

"Real meat and potatoes?" He asked.

"Yes."

"No more mush and dried foods?"

"No."

"Red meat and cholesterol and..." He laughed

at the quizzical look on Diana's face. "Hallelujah!" He cried. He took her hand as he marched them to the house.

Edward was amazed at how much the man could eat. He seemed to have no end to the amount he could put away. Edward cooked more meat to satisfy William's appetite. But, he finally slowed down , then pushed himself away from the table. Edward and Diana were watching him in amusement.

"Forgive me," he said, wiping his mouth with a napkin. "I haven't had a real meal in a long time. I will probably be sick most of the night because I couldn't get enough."

"Perhaps you should sleep in the barn, if you anticipate being sick," Diana suggested.

"Thank you," he smiled. "I'm also hoping there will be a real bed in this house."

"You're tired of the ground and floors already?" She asked.

"Is that how she's treated you?" Edward asked, with a look of mock sternness toward his niece. His eyes belied his feelings, for they twinkled with amusement.

"Unfortunately, Sir that's the only accommodations offered by our last dwelling." William came to Diana's defense. "And since our wedding, we have been traveling without the benefit of modern motels. But, she has hinted at a better life to come."

"Please stop calling me Sir and call me Edward, William. I feel so old when you treat me with that much respect."

Diana laughed. "And we get to call him Will, Uncle. He's our very own Will."

Edward laughed now, too, only a little more reserved. "I haven't heard this girl laugh like that since she was a child." He said. "This new life is going to be a delicious part of our lives. You, Dear Boy, have brought joy to my old age."

After a few good night's sleep and a day or two to recuperate, William found that there was much to do. Edward had the house built with four bedrooms and an addition for himself. There was an upper floor that housed two of the bedrooms. An upstairs was a luxury Diana had never seen. True to the tradition of the people in the valley city, Edward had put a pump in the kitchen of the house. Diana couldn't believe she had water in her own kitchen. "Someday, I'll build you a water closet," Will promised. She had no idea what it was, but his description sounded almost too good to be true. There would be no trips outside for water or, well, for <u>any</u>thing!

They fashioned one of the downstairs bedrooms into a surgery for Will. He built in walls to make two examining rooms and an office. With help from Frederick and others, they built a new doorway and entry stoop. Diana made him a sign to put out by their driveway along the main road.

"Now, I only need patients," he commented. "Not that I hope for illness or injury, but it is how I hope to provide for our family."

"It will happen, Will. You are a good man. Soon others will see it and have confidence to come to you for their cures."

It finally happened. One of his first patients was a sister of Thomas Woodslee. She had broken her arm and her father brought her to the new physician. The two men talked long of the past and the future and the goodness of Edward Woodslee's son. It was the beginning of a lifelong friendship.

William went to the city often, and in company with Edward Woodslee met many people. He marveled at the way their civilization was progressing. The city was called Newtowne. The inhabitants seemed to all hope that the residents of New Brighton would someday incorporate with them, all becoming one people. Will was impressed with the people and the industry in the area. They still relied mostly on farming, but he could see how they were evolving toward modernizing. They had a cannery, a tannery, and a ironworks which completely intrigued him. It was exciting to be living the history he had read about as a boy, to see progress in its infancy.

Harvest season brought about a celebration. The people at New Brighton held their own day of thanksgiving to celebrate their bountiful harvest from their new fields. Then, they went to the week long celebration of the city. There were races and pony rides, dances and contests, and things never seen or heard of before. Everyone laughed and talked and had such a good time. A few of the village people wondered if Father Jonathan would be displeased with them for acting so merry, but the fun was infectious and they didn't wonder about austerity for very long.

As fall gave way to winter, Diana began thinking about Rachel, Thomas, and Father Jonathan. "Perhaps we should go check on them," she suggested.

"They'll be fine," Will assured her.

"But, I expected them long before this," she complained.

"Diana, let go," he said patiently. "Let them have their life."

The fall rains set in then, and talk of travel ceased. Snow would soon follow the rains and might even now be covering the hills and mountains around them. They prepared the valley for the winter to come, putting away the bounteous stores from their hearty harvest. Wood lots filled, hay stacks grew, and folks settled down to the chores which would keep them busy during the cold, snowy months.

* * * * * * * * * * * * * *

Life for Rachel was much different than when she had been entirely alone, hiding from the world. She didn't see Thomas or the Father very often, but she knew they were nearby. It was comforting to know she wasn't really alone. Thomas supplied them all with fresh meat and fish, and they planted a small garden together, near her house. There were some preserved seeds in the root cellar along with the potatoes and carrots, which were almost too soft to eat, but could be used for seed. As the summer wore on, Rachel took pride in her little garden. She hoed and pulled out the weeds, looking with satisfaction at her work. It flourished under her care.

She took long walks in the forest from time to time. She talked to her mother, but the fog stayed beyond the Forbidden Hills, and Rachel never went that far. Her mother never came back, and Rachel was somehow content to let her go, now, even though she still persisted in talking to her when she was walking alone. "Can you see my garden, Mother?" She asked. "Do you think Thomas is a handsome man?" She blushed at the question. "Well, I do." She admitted. "Someday, I think we shall make a life together. Is that wicked?" She shook her head. "It doesn't feel wicked, Mother. I, I don't feel wicked at all, anymore. Is it wrong to feel happy like I do?" There were no answers to her questions. But, somehow it didn't matter.

In the fall, the three of them began cutting firewood to add to their meager piles left from the previous residents and not consumed in the forest fires. They harvested their garden stores and prepared for the winter. Rachel dried venison and fish against the month or two when it would be hard to get fresh meat. She collected and dried a few herbs she could remember were good for winter sicknesses.

"You don't have to stay because I won't leave,

Thomas," she said one evening as they ate a meal together.

"I'm content enough," he said.

"Why won't you go?" Father Jonathan asked her. "If you don't mind my asking," he added.

"I, well, I'm not sure, now," she answered. "I didn't want to leave Mother, at first. But, she's gone, now."

"She'll always be with you in your heart, Child," he said kindly.

"I know," she nodded.

"I found some wheels Will Armstrong must have made, Father," Thomas changed the subject. "I think we can make a small wagon for the trip, when the time comes. It will take us most of the winter."

"What about harness for the horses?"

"There's enough of that around. Elias had quite a collection in this old barn."

"Grandfather used to take harness in trade for the furniture he built." Rachel said in her whispering voice. "We didn't need it, but he always felt people needed the furniture and he could perhaps trade the harness for something else. I think he did sometimes."

"He was a kind man," Father Jonathan commented.

They awoke to snow one morning, but it was gone by the evening. "I am going to make one trip to the valley," announced Thomas. "It will relieve those who are waiting and give us news to contemplate over the coming winter."

Rachel was surprised at the intensity of her feelings at the thought of Thomas leaving. "How long will you be gone?" She asked timidly.

"I will return before the first, lasting snow."

"Then, you need to get away soon," added Father Jonathan. "I've seen ice along the creek almost every day since that snow. Take word of my love for everyone and that I shall return in the spring, I think."

"You're going to leave us?" Rachel asked.

"Yes, Child." He thought for a moment. "I came here to make peace with the past. Soon, I must look toward the future. I belong with our people."

The weather turned warm while Thomas was gone, teasing them from thinking about the cold coming behind it. Rachel took her last long walk into the forest. "What do I do, Mother?" She asked. The wind sighed in the trees, but no voices answered her. She nestled on the ground against a rock, allowing the sun to warm her face. As she dozed, she dreamed a dream. She saw Mother in the distance, but she could never quite catch up to her. 'Wait for me!' She yelled at the retreating figure, but Mother kept going. In the dream Rachel turned around and saw Thomas walking away from her in the other direction. 'Don't leave me!' she called. Thomas stopped and when he turned, his hand was out toward her. 'Come home with me,' he said. But, she was afraid. She turned again and saw Father Jonathan. He was also walking away. 'Father!' She called out. He stopped, but didn't turn around, then he resumed his walking until he was swallowed up in a forest of people. She peered at them and could see many faces she recognized, but they somehow couldn't see her. 'Diana', she said. But, the face was soon lost in the crowd. She turned back toward Mother, but she was now far away and obscured by the fog. She wasn't waiting. Just before she disappeared, she seemed to turn around and wave at Rachel. Rachel turned again and looked at Thomas. He still stood, arm outstretched to her.

Rachel awoke and looked around herself at the hills and forest. "This is the last time I shall come to this hill," she whispered. She put her hands up and rubbed them over her face and head. The scars were diminished to almost nothing. She drew up her knees and laid her head against them. There she drifted off into another dream. Her grandmother was suddenly standing before her. 'What have I done?' Rachel cried, cowering before the black-clad figure. 'You were always there to remind me of who I was,' came the harsh, old voice. But, the hatred and malevolence were gone from the face. Instead, Sarah Stuart looked old and tired. 'I only wanted you to love me,' Rachel whimpered. 'I did,' came the surprising answer. 'I loved you more than anyone. It is why you survived for so long. Of all the evil I did, I couldn't bring myself to be rid of you until the end. By then, I was totally mad.' 'I forgive you, Grandmother,' Rachel said, sobbing. 'I love you and I forgive you.' The old woman smiled for the first time Rachel could ever remember. 'That alone, will condemn me to my fate,' she said and disappeared into a gray cloud.

Rachel lifted her head to see only the trees around her. The sun was still shining. Her face and knees were wet from her tears. "It is over," she whispered, nodding her head. She breathed deep of the pine-scented air. Then, she rose and walked slowly home, meandering through forest and meadow.

"I was worried sick!" Father Jonathan greeted her as she descended the hill and crossed the creek. "You were gone a very long time. I have supper ready."

She smiled gratefully at him. "Thank you, Father." She said.

* * * * * * * * * * * * * *

Diana and Will were surprised when Thomas showed up at their door, late in the season. Diana looked into the gathering dusk behind him and asked. "Is Rachel with you?"

"No, not this time," he shook his head. "I've come on a quick trip alone." He assured them that all was well in the old village. Rachel was progressing in her friendliness toward him and the Father. "She's not so withdrawn and afraid, now," he said. "But, she does still retreat into herself."

"Time will still do much for her," Will commented.

"Father Jonathan wants to come home in the spring," Thomas said. "He misses you all, but he

231

needed this time to come to peace with his past."

"We all have scars of some kind, don't we?" Diana asked of no one in particular.

"How long will you stay, Thomas?" Asked Diana's uncle.

"Only a few days. I must travel back before we have a staying snow that would close the road up on top." He indicated the western escarpment.

"Has there been snow up there?" Diana asked.

"Yes, that's what prompted me to come now. In a few short weeks we will not be able to travel at all."

"Do you have enough stores for winter?"

"We planted a garden and have meat dried and hanging. Yes, I believe we are ready. I'm taking some molasses with me and fresh corn. It will be a delightful addition to our supplies."

Thomas spent the next few days with his family. He teased his sister about her broken arm, accusing her of doing it just so she could be a patient of the handsome Will Avery. She blushed and blustered in denial. He marveled at the shop and house his father and others had completed for him. "It's a grand sight," he sighed. He looked at his father. "I'll be home in the spring."

"And will you bring us a new daughter?" Asked his mother.

He smiled sadly. "Perhaps, Mother," he answered. "I think, perhaps."

"Your father said that was your quest," she said quietly, wiping at a tear with her apron.

Thomas walked to her and put an arm lovingly around her shoulders. "We shall see, Mother," he said awkwardly. "If I come alone in the spring, it will not be to stay, you understand. Then someday I will bring you the daughter you so desire."

"Well, never mind," she said, pushing at him. "Your house is done and you will live there when you return." She smiled bravely. "You are a grown man, after all."

"I won't be far away, then," he consoled.

"It's just a good, long walk, Mother," offered her husband. "We can visit him often."

"And perhaps we can have nieces and nephews," offered Anna, his sister. "That is, if Charlotte doesn't beat you to a wedding!" She laughed merrily at the blush from her older sister.

"A wedding, Charlotte?" Thomas asked.

She laughed, shaking her head in denial, but not answering his question.

"So soon you all grow up!" Said his mother. "Two almost gone from the house already!"

"Yes," said his father in mock despair. "And we're left with only three daughters more!"

They all laughed, then rode in their wagon to the Woodslee home. There, Thomas took his leave from the family in the morning. Lowering clouds told of a storm approaching. "Rain for us, but no doubt snow for you, Son," were his father's parting words. Thomas rode up the steep trail, then stopped on top and waved. He could barely discern what he thought were his parents returning his greeting before he remounted his horse and headed back to the old village.

* * * * * * * * * * * * *

Winter was bitterly hard in the valley that season. The snow was deep and the temperatures dropped sharply. Will reinstated Christmas in the village. He added things Marianne had only touched upon. They celebrated together, remembering the things she had taught them, yet understanding more what the tradition was about. The holiday celebration spread quickly to the city, as well.

Will traded his doctoring skills for gifts for his family. The most surprising gift of all was a cradle he bought for one of the bedrooms he termed 'the nursery'. Diana was delighted to tell him of her impending pregnancy. He was so excited. "I never knew there could be this kind of joy in the world," she confided to her uncle one day. "Will is so full of life and love!"

"After all those sad years," he said. "How fitting it is to watch the blessings of a good life for you, and for us all."

If the winter was hard in the valley, it was most difficult upon the mountain. The snow was heavy and deep. They didn't have the wind from off the river to drive their temperatures quite so low as in the valley, but it was cold, indeed. Thomas and Father Jonathan had to tramp the snow down in the corral for the horses to have a place to move around. They dug and tramped a path to the root cellar so they could get to their food. They all ended up staying at Rachel's home because the snow was too bad to travel up to the houses on the hills. They spent days on end without relief, cooped up in the tiny house. Thomas taught them to play the game of Draughts which whiled away many hours.

"I have seriously changed my perspective on what is important in life," Father Jonathan announced one day. "Love and happiness are the most important things, after all, I've decided. And family." They all heartily agreed.

Spring finally came. The snow began to melt into streams which soon became rivers everywhere. The sun felt warm again instead of just bright. One morning, when most of the snow was gone, Rachel ventured down to the creek to pluck some pussy willows for the house. The creek was overrunning its banks and looked like a big pool. As she bent over the water to pull at the plants, she saw her reflection in the water. She stopped and stared. Her left hand came up automatically to her face. Then, she dropped her twigs and put her right hand up, also. She bent closer to the water. The sun was shining brightly and she could see herself clearly. She closed her left eye. The cloudiness was gone and she could see with her right eye. The images weren't completely clear, but she could see. She looked up at the sky and trees around her. With both eyes, she could see most clearly. She looked down into the water once again and marveled at the smoothness of her face. The right side was still red, but it wasn't ugly to look at. The skin felt only a little rough. Suddenly, she began to laugh and cry all at the same time. It was a miracle! She balled her fists and pressed them against her mouth. It was a miracle!

Her hair was parted on the left and brushed across her head. She drew it back to reveal the scars and lack of hair on the right. Her damaged ear was small, but not so bad to look at as when it was a scarred knob. The scars were still visible on her head, but not in lumps and ridges as before. She let her hair drop back into place, then smoothed it over her ears and caught it back, winding it into a bun at the back of her neck. *I look like my mother!* She gasped. The tears flowed then. She sat back on the ground and let them flow. *I can see her wherever I go! She will always be with me!* She sobbed then, into her drawn-up knees, her hair forgotten. "Good-bye, Mother," she whispered. Yet, her whisper had more voice to it than before. She cleared her throat and talked in a low voice. "When he asks again I shall go, but I shall never forget you," she said. "I know I carry you with me inside and out, wherever I go." *I know now that you have always been there,* she thought. With that, she rose from the damp ground and picked up the twigs she'd dropped, turning to walk back to the house. It was empty. The men had gone to the back of the barn to put the finishing touches on the wagon. Rachel decorated the table with the pussy willow twigs she'd gathered. She hummed a tune as she cleaned the small living quarters. Her voice gave out after only a short time, but she could hum! She had a voice again, after all this time. She wondered idly how long she had been able to speak in this new sultry voice. *While I was impatiently waiting for the healing to come, it just came without my noticing,* she smiled as she worked.

In the evening, Rachel asked Thomas and Father Jonathan if they wanted to walk with her.

Thomas looked up at her in surprise. "Yes," he breathed his answer.

Father Jonathan wisely declined. "You children go on ahead," he said. "I'm feeling rather tired this evening."

They walked the length of the village and back to the road toward the river. It too, was running high they noticed as they approached its banks. "Mother once asked why we didn't travel on the river," she commented, looking askance of Thomas.

"We could," he said. "But, a few miles down river is a waterfall of great height. If we didn't get sucked into the current and go over, it would be a treacherous climb down the side. The boats would have to be left behind."

"And the other way?" She asked.

"There are some very swift rapids that would be impossible to navigate going up river." He said.

"Does the river go to our valley?" She asked.

He looked at her sharply. *Had she just said 'our valley'?* He recovered quickly. "Yes. At the south end of the valley it is wide and beautiful. We fish there, and use boats, and we use the water to irrigate our fields."

"What does that mean?" She asked, frowning slightly.

"Irrigation?"

She nodded without answering.

"We channel the water from the river into ditches and let it spread over our fields. It waters them the whole summer so our crops are fruitful nearly every year."

"It sounds like heaven," she said.

He smiled and slipped his hand into hers. They walked back to the village, briefly stopping to peer down on the grave of her grandmother. Rachel told Thomas of her dream up on the mountain while he had been gone before winter.

"You have found your own peace this winter," he said.

"I have," she nodded. "I have healed in many ways." Her right hand came up to touch her face lightly.

"The scars are almost gone," he commented.

"Inside and out," she answered.

"Your voice is stronger."

"Yes!" She said with delight. Then, for no reason at all, she laughed. It was a throaty laugh that brought tears to her face. She was surprised to

238

see tears streaming down Thomas' face as well. But, he was smiling, too.

"It's time to go home, Rachel," he said.

"I know," she nodded, still smiling.

He took her into his arms and kissed her. Her arms fell lovingly around his shoulders. "Father Jonathan will be pleased," she said into his neck.

He pushed her back to arms length. "Father Jonathan?" He said. "He isn't going to be half as pleased as Diana and Will and my family." He pushed her hair from her face. "They are waiting for us there, Rachel. They are waiting for a new sister. I can't begin to tell you how excited they will be when we arrive."

Fear gripped her for a moment. She started to pull away. But, she suddenly remembered her reflection in the pool at the creek. *I have nothing to fear,* she thought. It did little to relieve her panic, but Thomas drew her to him and held her tight. That helped.

"Wait!" She said, pushing away from him. She drew her hair back as she had at the creek. "Do you like my hair this way?" She asked.

Thomas started to laugh. "What?" He said. At the look of dismay in her eyes, he stopped. "I do like it, Rachel." He said, turning her around to see what she was doing with it. He faced her again. "It makes you look older."

"Is that good?"

"Yes, it's fine."

"Will I scare them?" She asked, letting her hair drop.

"No," he said. "You will charm them as you have me."

She smiled. "Then, let's go home before I change my mind." She said as she started down the road away from him.

He strode to her and turned her to him for another kiss. "Yes, let's go home," he breathed against her forehead. As they walked, he chattered like a school boy. "Wait until you see our house. My father and others finished it over the summer, while we were here. And my shop! I can hardly wait to go to work in my new shop. It isn't large, but my father thought it was quite big." He stopped in both words and stride, turning to look at her. She smiled at him, then they laughed together, continuing to walk to the house.

Father Jonathan watched them go with some worry. He thought Rachel had come to some decision this day. She had cleaned and decorated the house and seemed light of mood. It wasn't like her to be outgoing, but she seemed to be just that at supper. When she suggested the walk, he knew she really wanted to speak to Thomas alone. But, he feared what she would say. She might be ready to get rid of them. Would she send them packing down the road soon? He went into the woods behind the house and prayed while they were gone. He poured out his own healed soul to his God and asked for forgiveness for all his follies. He pled for his people so far away in their new valley. He asked that Rachel and Thomas would make a good decision about the future. Peace flooded over him and when he emerged, back to the house, he was witness to the laughter of the two young people. *All is well,* he thought. *My prayers are answered.*

"Shall we marry before we leave as William and Diana did?" Asked Thomas.

"Oh, no!" Said the monk. "The entire village will want to be witness to this union!" He shook a finger at them. "Please, let us wait until we get to the valley."

Thomas turned to Rachel. "Is that how you feel?" He asked.

She thought for what seemed like a very long time. "Yes," she finally whispered. Then, clearing her throat, she talked in her new voice. "I think it is the right thing to do."

"Wouldn't it please your family?" Father Jonathan asked of Thomas.

"You're right!" He answered. "My mother and sisters wouldn't soon forgive me if I denied them the fun of preparing for a wedding. They will want to fuss over you, Rachel."

She bit her lip in apprehension. "I'll try to be patient with them, but I am afraid of others still, Thomas."

"They will take you in as another daughter and sister, Rachel," Thomas promised.

"I've met them and they are a delightful family. You are so lucky, Rachel. God is smiling on you."

"Thank you," she said as she patted his hand, holding firmly to Thomas with her other one.

They spent two days preparing to leave. When it came right down to it, Rachel still held back for a whole day while she and Thomas rode horses to Diana's old home and then to the Armstrong cabin so she could say good-bye. She looked at the grave markers for a long time, touching each one. "This is the only family I have to offer you, Thomas," she said sadly.

"Isn't Diana family?" He asked.

She thought for a moment, then nodded. "Yes, a cousin."

"Then, we'll concentrate on your living relations and let these rest," he suggested.

She smiled, then. As they remounted their horses, she said. "Let's leave tomorrow."

And so they did. It took them three days of pushing the horses along the muddy trail to get to the top of the escarpment. Rachel breathed in the sight, from the city on the left to the glassy river on the right. "Where is our home?" She asked Thomas.

He pointed to their house and shop sitting by itself along the road between the city and the village. "If you look closely toward the eastern slope," he said, pointing beyond their home. "You'll just see the roof of the house where Diana and Will and Edward Stuart live. There behind those trees and boulders."

Rachel clapped her hands. "Oh, and I see the chapel, too, Father!" She said to the monk who had opted to stay seated on the wagon. He nodded pleasantly in response. Rachel turned back to look at the vista once again. Thomas slipped an arm around her. "Can they see us?" She asked.

"If they're looking, but the light is fading behind us, so we may not be very visible."

She smiled and hugged Thomas. "Home," she said against his cheek. "We're home."

"Yes," he said, hugging her back.

They got back into the wagon and headed down the trail to the valley floor. As they came around onto the road, Rachel stood up. "Stop, Thomas!" She said. She breathed deeply, smelling the earthiness of the valley mixed with the fishy smell of the nearby river. "Yes," she said, sitting back. "New Brighton, at last!"

Nine

The Shadow Land and Beyond

Thomas first stopped to let Father Jonathan off at his new chapel. Then he drove to Diana's home where amid cries and laughter, he arranged for Rachel to stay until a wedding could be planned and executed. Reluctantly, he left her there, standing with Diana on the porch, and drove to his own home. He walked through the empty barn and shop, then walked through the rooms of the spacious, new house. He envisioned Rachel and himself, surrounded by children, living their lives in this spot. He looked out a window and pictured a garden in the dooryard. He thought of what it would be like to come into the kitchen and sit with his own family to eat supper, then tell stories to them before bed. He remembered sitting with his sisters, listening as his father told them stories, with his mother interjecting a thing or two. He took one more look around, then, he climbed back aboard the wagon and drove to the home of his parents. They were both delighted and relieved to see him.

"Your mother has had me check your house everyday lately for your return. I told her you would come here, but..." He raised his hands in resignation.

Thomas hugged his mother and each of his sisters. "I see you are still at home, Charlotte," he commented.

She bowed her head. "He still hasn't asked me to marry him," she answered, then looked up with a smile. "But, he will!"

"Here, come and eat," urged his mother. "You must be hungry for real food after your trip. You look thin to me."

Thomas allowed himself to be waited upon and answered as many questions as he could about winter up on the mountain, while eating. He basked in the love of his family. When he had finished eating, he began a sort of family council. "Everyone gather around the table," said he. "We need to talk about your new sister." There were excited squeals and laughter, and soon he was surrounded by the attentive faces of those he loved. "Rachel Stuart is her name," he paused, a slight smile gracing his face. "For now," he added. "She and I have found love and will be wed as soon as those arrangements can be made."

"Why didn't she come with the others? Why haven't we gotten to meet her family?" Asked his younger sister, Anna. "Where is she now?"

"You've already met Diana, her cousin." He examined his hands in front of him on the table.

"Most of her family is dead, but she does have Diana and Edward. She is staying with them right now." Now he looked at each of their faces in turn. "It is not something to discuss with her, the subject of her family. Not now, perhaps not ever. We," he made a circle with his hands. "We, will be her family."

"Does this have to do with Mary?" Asked his mother.

Thomas nodded. "It does, but we will speak of that another time. Rachel is <u>not</u> Mary, if that is your concern."

His mother nodded, relief flooding her face.

"Your mother and I have talked of this, Thomas. We are sure you have made a right decision, but it's hard for parents to allow their children freedom all at once. We've been preparing ourselves while you were gone over the winter, but we still want to guide you, if we may."

"I know, Father," Thomas acknowledged. "I appreciate all of your counsel."

"When will we meet Rachel?" Charlotte asked. "I'm ready for a new sister. These old ones are about worn out." The seriousness of the conversation was broken and they all laughed easily together.

"We're worn out?" Cried one of the others. "Ha! You're the one who isn't fun anymore, always moping around for your beau. It will be good for the rest of us when you are married and gone to your own home!" Charlotte stuck out her tongue at her sister, then smiled sweetly.

"Girls!" Chided their mother.

Thomas laughed. "It's good to be home," he said. "But, now I must get some sleep. Perhaps I can persuade Rachel to meet one or two of you tomorrow. She's shy. Please, be patient with her."

"We know of her injuries, Son," said his mother. "We have spoken of it to the girls so there won't be any surprises. We're ready to meet her on her own terms and in her own way."

"Thank you, Mother."

It took only a few days for the wedding plans to come to fruition. The little chapel was filled to overflowing with the friends of the bride and the family and friends of the groom. Father Jonathan positively beamed and glowed at the prospect of performing the service. There was a grand party at Diana's home before the happy couple went to their own, newly furnished house.

Rachel was exhausted. It was the first time she had been in public, and what a lot of public it was! She alternately felt that everyone was staring at her or deliberately not looking at her at all. She didn't know which was worse. But, now she could relax in the privacy of her own home. That too, lasted for only a few days. Her new family couldn't stay away for long.

Thomas' sisters fussed over Rachel and made her feel like one of the family from the first day they met her. Being much the same age, they shared clothes and shoes with her. Charlotte gently showed her many hair styles that would effectively hide her scars yet still look elegant. Rachel was surprised at how easily she became attached to Thomas' family. They were fun and kind. His mother was a warm, wonderful woman. She wasn't nearly as frightening as Rachel had imagined. "I thought she might be like Grandmother," she confided to Diana one evening. "But, she is more like your mother."

Some of the attention showered on Rachel was before the wedding, but most of it was afterward. They all spent time with her, but it was Anna and Rachel who became best friends. Anna would come to her house and help Rachel with daily chores while Thomas worked in his shop or in their fields. They went riding together and walking, too. Anna took Rachel to the city, but it was too frightening. "I'm from a very small village, Anna," she explained. "This is too much for me!" They left, but not before Anna bought some peppermint sticks for them. Rachel had to agree that the taste was divine.

She was still a little fearful of Thomas' parents, but was learning that they were kindly and only wanted to help her set up her new home with their son. His mother helped her cook, giving her new ideas on meals and their preparation. She was older and caused Rachel's heart to beat faster for fear she would reprimand her if she made a mistake. It didn't take long however, for Rachel to see that her new mother was full of patience and laughter. When Rachel dropped a whole bowl full of eggs, they laughed and laughed as they cleaned up the mess. Thomas' mother confessed to spilling a whole meal onto the table while everyone watched in horror. "This is much better than that day, Rachel," she said amid her laughter and tears. "We can clean it up together and no one else ever needs to know."

Now when tears sprang to Rachel's eyes, they were those of gratitude and gaiety, not fear and dread. She began slowly to enter into conversations and offer some part of herself to these kind people.

Rachel realized how much she had to learn to be a good wife. Her homemaking skills were woefully lacking when compared to even the youngest of the Woodslee sisters. She avidly copied their styles and ways of dressing and cleaning and cooking. They patiently taught her to stitch and quilt. She made feather ticks for their bed when the neighbors held a feather party. Thomas often complimented her on her efforts. As all of these people accepted her, confidence in herself grew and replaced the old fears. Thomas put a mirror in their bedroom and she could look into it to brush her hair and not look away.

Diana had given birth to a little girl whom they named Marianne. She was a delightful, happy child, mirroring the beauty of her mother. Rachel was fascinated with the baby and she and Anna would often take her for walks and tend her for Diana. That is, when Diana and Will were willing to let the child go. Everyone, it seems, loved Marianne.

Soon, Rachel herself, told the family that she and

Thomas would also have a child. Together, she and Thomas dreamed and envisioned what it would be like to be parents, and Rachel watched even more closely what it took to raise a child. She wanted their child to be happy, but feared that she would overindulge the infant. "Can a child be too happy?" She asked Thomas' mother.

"I don't think so," she answered. " But you can spoil a child by giving too much. They must learn to hear the word 'no' sometimes. And work, they must learn the value of work to be truly happy when they grow up. Although they will complain all the while,"she confided.

Rachel and Thomas agreed that if the baby was a girl, they would name her Ruth, after Rachel's natural mother. If it were a boy, he would be named Elijah, for her father. Life in New Brighton was happy for them all, at last. The memories of earlier, darker days were beginning to fade for everybody.

* * * * * * * * * * * * *

Frederick Wilder and George Bays watched from their logging sight as the fog crept closer and closer toward them. It was still miles away, but each day during the summer it seemed to be nearer. It didn't dissipate, but hung in the hills and valleys day after day. In the distance, on a clear day, they could see the high mountain peaks beyond the old village, but between them and the mountaintops, the fog loomed as a barrier. It looked like a vast, cloudy sea, separating them from the rest of the world. Time seemed to stand still for them in their hidden valley. "Perhaps Will is right," Frederick said. "Perhaps the rest of the world goes on without us. Perhaps we're stuck here in this world."

"Did you ever think we might be in another world?" George asked.

"The shadow land?"

"No, I was thinking of a land away from the shadows."

"Hm," Frederick grunted. "Then Will must be from a land beyond the shadows."

They looked again at the fog-shrouded valleys between their escarpment and the mountains of the Forbidden Ridge. Soon after this conversation, they packed up their tools and went home.

* * * * * * * * * * * * * *

Anita Wallick awoke from her fevered dreams. She was in familiar surroundings, the blue walls of her room taking on shape as she came more fully to consciousness. She became aware of the I V line in her left arm and looked at the monitor with its dripping bag of solution hanging near her. She sat up and swung her feet to the floor.

A nurse scurried to her side. "You're awake!" She said loudly.

"Obviously," Anita muttered.

"What can I do for you?" The nurse busied herself with the drip monitor, then turned to smile brightly at her patient, smoothing the rumpled sheet and blanket.

"I'm not sure," Anita sighed. "I'm not sure why I'm here. Why don't you tell me?"

"Well, the doctor will be in soon," answered the nurse vaguely.

"Of course." Anita nodded. "May I just get up and walk to the window?"

"Certainly. Let me help you in case you're dizzy."

"Why should I be dizzy?" Anita looked around her, then back at the nurse. "How long have I been here?"

"A few days. Don't you remember? You've been up walking before."

Anita stared at her, dumbfounded. *A few days?* She took another look around her room. This wasn't the hospital, as she had first thought. *Where am I, then?* She thought with a deep frown. "Where am I?" She repeated her thought.

"Don't get agitated, Ma'am," the girl admonished. "Just relax. You've been very ill."

"Ill with what?" Anita demanded, then sighed. "Why don't you send me someone who knows something?" She'd dealt with too many patients, been a nurse herself, too long. She knew this young nurse, or aide, or whatever she was, didn't really know anything.

"I, I'll go see what's keeping the doctor." The girl

fled from the room before Anita could ask any more questions.

Anita stood carefully. She was a little light-headed, but not really dizzy. She grabbed hold of the rolling monitor, then walked the few steps to the window where she looked out upon a beautifully landscaped lawn. She leaned heavily on the wide window sill. Her legs did feel a little weak. *I must have been here for quite a little while,* she mused as she peered at the sight outside. There were people in wheel chairs and others sitting on benches and at tables. She watched for a moment as nurses in white dresses fussed over each person.

"Hello, Anita," floated a soft voice from the doorway behind her.

She turned to face Doctor Jones. "At last, a familiar face!" She proclaimed. "How are you, Doctor Jones?"

He smiled and walked to her side to shake her hand. "More to the point, how are you?"

"Well, of that, I'm not sure, it seems." She smiled back at him.

"Let's sit, shall we?" He indicated the two chairs near the window.

"I'm in Parkview," she stated as she slid easily into the chair. "Why is that?"

"Can you recall the discussions we've already had?" He asked.

That took her aback. She stared at him for a moment, then looked toward the window. All she could see from her chair were the tops of the trees and a partly cloudy sky. He sat patiently, waiting while she searched her mind for answers. *What's wrong with me?* She thought. *I am in a psychiatric home and I don't know why! What have I done? What's happened to me?* She scratched her head, for the first time noticing the bandage over her left ear. "Have I been injured?" She asked, totally confused.

"Yes," he nodded. "You have suffered a head injury. Do you remember how it happened?"

"No," she said simply. "How long have I been here?" She asked after a long pause.

"About two months, Anita." Was the astonishing reply.

"And I've had amnesia of some kind?"

"It would seem so. You've had difficulty remembering even simple things until now. What I'm seeing today is much better. However I must warn you, you've had lucid days before this, only to relapse."

"It must be the fog," she muttered.

"Excuse me?" He queried.

"Nothing." She shook her head gently. "Have I lost my job?" She asked.

"You're on suspension, I believe. Until you gain back your memory and your strength."

"Suspension? Not leave?" She asked in concern.

"Well, there are a few details that need cleared up. We'll do that in time. I don't want you to overtax yourself, so if you are the least agitated or feeling exhaustion, we'll quit talking so you can rest. Agreed?"

"Yes," she nodded. "How was I injured?"

"We believe you fell."

"You believe?"

He splayed his hands before her, but didn't answer.

"Doctor Avery and I went..." Thoughts, pictures, memories of fog and mountains flooded into her mind. The details weren't clear, but there was enough to frighten her. She looked sharply at the psychiatrist seated near her. "Where is Doctor Avery?" She asked abruptly.

He stroked his chin, watching her carefully. "I hope you will tell me that little detail." He said. "You say the two of you went somewhere. Do you remember?"

Her stomach churned with a nameless fear. Instinctively, she knew they had been over this ground before. There was something wrong, but she couldn't put it into words. She stared out the window, willing the trees to convey her thoughts into palpable words. "Can't he tell you? Why isn't he here helping me remember?" Her voice came out like that of a little girl. She swallowed hard. "Has he been injured, as well?"

"Why don't you just tell me what you do remember, and we'll piece it together bit by bit?"

But, she suddenly wanted only to sleep. "I think

I need to lie down," she said wearily.

"That's fine," he said, helping her into her bed. "I'll come back this evening and we'll talk again. But, he didn't leave the room. Instead, he sat in the chair and waited until she fell into a troubled sleep.

When Anita awoke sometime in the afternoon, she felt more rested. She called for a nurse to help her wash and comb her hair. She walked to the bathroom, then a little ways down the hallway before sitting in her room to await supper. Doctor Jones came into her room as she was finishing her meal. She didn't wait for him to prompt her. With a sigh, she began. "We, William Avery and I, went on a camping trip." She looked around the room as though gathering her thoughts. "We were lost in the fog for days and days."

"Just the two of you?" He asked.

"Why, no!" She stopped and stared at the doctor. "We, uh," she sighed again. "We had Marianne Armstrong with us. But, you knew that, didn't you?"

"You've mentioned it a time or two. Is this the girl who was found during the forest fires, the one we thought might be from the missing plane?"

"Yes."

"Go on." He looked at her carefully.

"Well, we were lost and wandering around for days, like I said. It was wet in the forest and we slipped and fell on the wet grass. Then he, William, fell into a creek and got wet through and through.

From that he got pneumonia or bronchitis, or both. He was so sick!" She looked up, suddenly frightened. She rubbed her hands over her head in agitation. "Oh, no!" She shook her head and put her hands to her mouth. "I was supposed to bring help to him. I started back to the car from our campsite, but it was gone. Has anyone gone up there to check on him? Have I told you any of this before?"

"We'll discuss that later, but not if you're going to get upset. Breathe deeply to calm yourself. Right now if you can, I need you to tell me your story. You're giving me more detail than you have before." Again, he waited.

"That's all I remember," she said and became quiet.

The doctor waited for several minutes before he finally cleared his throat and began telling her a story. "You were found by hikers about two months ago at the bottom of a very steep cliff. It seems you had fallen. Your injuries were mostly superficial, scrapes and scratches, except for the skull fracture and concussion. You were unconscious for a very long time, bordering on coma. Since you woke up, you have been in various states of delirium and depression. You've called for Doctor Avery. You've called for this, Marianne. You've tried to escape."

He stopped for a moment while she gained control of her emotions. Her face was wet with the flood of tears she endured. She shook her head as she held her face in her hands. "You did tell us about your quest of help for Doctor Avery. There was a manhunt for him and Miss Armstrong, but to no avail. They have effectively disappeared. And you could tell us no more that helped in the search."

"I think I can show you where I last left them if someone will drive me out to our original campsite." Anita offered.

"I don't know if that's a possibility, but I will look into it. It seems to me that a trip out there is what started all this business." He waved a hand to dismiss the thought. "Well, be that as it may, you must know that a skeleton has just recently been found. That is, parts of it have been found. Some large animal has had its way with it, so there's not much left. I believe the police are assuming it to be that of Doctor Avery."

A great silence filled the room. The news shocked Anita into an utter void. No thoughts would come, only a blank. She sat in a stupor for some moments. *William, dead?* She finally thought. *I left him there and she let him die?* With great difficulty, she responded to the voice of the doctor.

"Anita?" He was kneeled before her, shaking her arm gently. "Are you with me?"

She nodded. "Yes. Yes, I'm fine, I'm fine." She looked at him, then away at the floor. "Are you sure it's William?" She asked weakly.

"The authorities seem pretty sure." He sat back in his chair. "Is there anything else you can tell me? Any details that might help us clear you of this?"

"Clear me?" She frowned. "What do you mean? Surely no one thinks I did anything wrong?"

"We just don't know what happened out there." He explained.

"Let me think." She stated. After a short pause, she looked up at the doctor sadly. "May we talk again another time? I believe I would like to sleep now."

The doctor left her with a promise that he would be back early in the morning. True to his word, he appeared as she was finishing her breakfast. She began her tale again. "We, William and I, took Marianne up to see if the mountains would help her with her memory." She laughed slightly. "I think the fog does something to people's minds up there. Anyway, she led us around and around in circles, over one ridge after another. We tied string to some trees and bushes. That's how we found out we were really going around in circles. William fell into a stream, and we were already wet from the fog and misty weather. We couldn't get dry, or warm. He began coughing, then having fevers. I treated him with medicine he had in his bag, but some of that stuff had gotten wet in his floundering around in the water. Finally, we came back around full circle and I told him I would go for help. The car was only a couple of miles away, we were sure." She paused for several minutes. "I remember climbing up to the top of a rocky hill and looking down at our old campsite. The car was gone. I wondered why no one had looked for us."

"They had," he interrupted. "That's why the car was gone. A search was done soon after you first didn't come back to work. The rain and mists worked against them finding tracks that would have helped in finding you sooner." She nodded in acknowledgment.

During the pause, she had time to reflect and gain confidence in her memory. She sighed deeply as she began once again. "Then I remember walking down the roadway until long after dark. I was exhausted, feeling a little sick myself. I just wanted to find a place to lie down and rest. I finally went into a growth of trees to sleep on some moss for the night." She held up her hands. "That's it. That's all I remember."

He nodded, pulling at his chin in thought. "It's consistent with what we do know. The trauma of the fall would probably blot out any memory of that fact. You were found about ten or so miles from your old campsite. There were trees at the top of the cliff, near the road. You might have just walked off the cliff."

"I shouldn't have left him, I guess," she said sadly. "We just thought it was our only hope of getting help." She snorted softly. "Hope," was all she said.

"You couldn't know there would be an accident."

"No-o-o, but what happened him? To Marianne?"

"We don't know. There's just no sign of her at all." He smiled broadly at her. "I'm pleased with the return of your memory at last, Anita. I know the police will be, too. I'll sit in with you on any conferences you have with them. And, I'll see to it that you have a good attorney to help you, too. I think they will be very satisfied with you, now."

"I suppose it will take all of that," she said, her voice sounding dull and tired suddenly.

"I'm sorry about Doctor Avery," he said. "I know you were close friends."

"Yes," she said. "Thank you."

"It will be over before you know it and you'll be able to go home. Now that you're coming back to yourself, I think you'll be out of here quickly." He paused. "You did the best you could. No one can ever foresee an accident. It isn't your fault that you couldn't get back to the camp. Don't dwell on the pains and sorrows. I'll be here to help you work through your grief, then you can look forward."

"Two months!" She breathed. "I suppose there's no hope at all for either of them. They wouldn't have had enough food, or any way to produce more. Marianne always found something, but it wasn't enough. It was never enough."

"Do you know where she was leading you?" He asked.

She laughed ruefully. "Nowhere," she answered. "Nowhere at all."

"By the way," he said as a thought struck him. "Why did you take Miss Armstrong's hospital records with you?" He asked.

She frowned. "We didn't. That is, I didn't. I can't imagine why William would have done that. He surely would have told me. No! There's just no reason to do that! I'm sure he didn't."

"We haven't been able to find any files for her. She wasn't really one of my patients, so I didn't have a file on her. I gave all my theories and speculations to William when we held that conference with the Kincaid family."

"There's nothing?" She asked, a bewildered look on her face.

"Nothing. No admittance, no discharge, no medicines, nothing. I've had quite a time convincing the police there was such a person."

"Isn't that strange?" She mused. "William kept saying that it was almost as if she didn't exist at all, that we were following a phantom through the fog." She paused. "She did exist, didn't she?"

He shook his head. "I've wondered that, myself. Almost no one at the hospital remembers her. I managed to find one newspaper article that mentioned when they found her. The men who found her weren't real firemen, just volunteers who could have been from anywhere. They, of course, cannot be found."

"What of the Kincaid's?"

"Their daughter's body was accounted for when they found the wreckage of the airplane."

"I don't believe in phantoms, do you?" She asked.

He rose, shaking his head. "Well, don't think about it too much. We've done more than enough for today." He moved toward the door. "You can walk, eat, have a shower. I'll get someone to take that drip off for you. If I don't see you tomorrow, I'll be back on Friday. Then, we'll talk about discharge." He started out the door, then looked back in at her. "By the way, welcome home."

She smiled thinly, then laid back on her bed. She felt suddenly very, very tired. She lay there, thinking of William and Marianne. *She wouldn't have left him,* she thought. *I can't believe he's dead. Really, she took more pains with him than she did with me.* After a few moments, the thought became a conviction in her heart. She smiled at the clouds outside her window. *Fare thee well, William. Wherever she's led you, fare thee well. Many things may have happened, but your death is not one of them.* She shook her head in new confidence. *Well, let them have their 'facts'. I think I'm beginning to understand why I had to be the one to return. She wasn't leading us, just you. I know that somewhere you are alive and happy still. Perhaps I do believe in phantoms, after all.* She drifted into an easy sleep, smiling. "Good-bye, William," she muttered as she faded away to happy dreams.

* * * * * * * * * * * * * *

A quiet council was held in the chapel at New Brighton. Father Jonathan called the meeting to order and allowed Frederick Wilder to tell his tale.

He stood awkwardly to address the small assembly of men. "We have been watching for many days as the old fog of the Forbidden Hills creeps closer. It looks now like it has stopped just a few miles from us, between us and the old village." He looked at George Bays, who nodded his agreement. "It doesn't move or fade like fog usually does when the sun shines. It just sits there like a forbidding cloud in the trees."

"What do you make of this?" Asked Edward Woodslee.

"Will Armstrong used to advise us to never cross the fog. He showed us the deep valley of fog in the Forbidden Hills. On the other side of it, he said, was a world beyond our reckoning. Over the years, we have seen some of the things of which he spoke. Nothing which penetrated to us from that fog has lasted in our world, as we know it, except for Brother Avery, of course. We assume we couldn't last in their world either, wherever that is." He paused. "Now, the fog has taken over our old valley. It was a place of much pain and heartache. Perhaps the fog will heal all the torments of that land. Now that Thomas and his family are with us," he nodded at the younger man. "And Father Jonathan has also come home, there is no reason for us to venture beyond our own valley and supporting forest. All of our people and all we possess is here, in this prosperous valley. The fog may only be a reminder that we cannot go back. We, George and I," he nodded to his friend, who again agreed. "Have no desire to do so. That is our story." He sat down heavily on his chair, next to his friend.

Edward Woodslee spoke from his seat. "There is another large town to our north about a day's journey away. They have traded with us for many years. To the south and the east are Indian villages and other smaller settlements. We also trade with them. Sometimes we have conflicts, but usually we have peace, and barter when and what we can. We have no real need to travel west, for now." There was general agreement from the assembly.

Father Jonathan stood to add a few words. "There are some superstitions and fears that have cropped up from the incidents of the past few years in our old home. The cause of most of those stories and horrors is gone. After the fires, the fear grew, but I believe we have overcome that fright. In this valley I hope we can put all of that to rest, but I suspect that this fog will cause some new gossip of shadows and haunts in the old village. There might be stories of shadowy presences coming down the road, to scare the children." He looked around the room. "And a few adults as well. I suppose there is no way to stop that kind of thing, but I feel that if there is just no reason to go up the western escarpment, then there is no reason for stories to grow out of the fog." He sat down and indulged the murmuring of many voices.

"There's plenty of wood to the north," offered Thomas loudly to overcome the general conversation.

"We don't need to go up on top to cut trees. That's really the only reason we go up there, now. Herbs grow in plenty, here in the valley."

"Aye," agreed his father. "We could destroy the road to the top." Again, there was a lot of low talking and muttering as the men digested the news and speculated on Thomas' words, and those of his father.

"Let's do it, then!" Someone called out.

"Aye!" Came an answering voice. "Let's let the past die and look forward. If it means cutting off that old road, so be it! There's been too many accidents on that steep hillside, as it is."

There was a clamor of voices to forge ahead with the plan. They took a vote and agreed to break up the treacherous track up the mountain.

William Avery sat at the back of the room, listening as the townsfolk discussed their issues. He had no suggestions. He was ready to be divorced from his old life and fully live his new one. He would take part in community affairs when they no longer dealt with the old, but centered on the current events of New Brighton. There was nothing left for him in the 'outside' world now. He felt a small pang of regret as he thought of Anita Wallick, but knew she would have already dealt with whatever situation was facing her in the 'outside'. It had been many months, even 'outside'. *No, that part of my life is over and Diana and Marianne are my future,* he told himself. A smile stole across his face as he pictured his old friend. *Good-bye, Dear Anita. May you leave the past as I have and find your new future.* He came out of his reverie and discovered he was much happier as a physician in the seventeenth century, if that's where he was, than he had been as a rather wealthy doctor in the twentieth century, where he had been born. He breathed deeply and watched his friends as they planned to cut themselves off from the western world. He smiled and nodded as those around him tried to drag him into the conversation, but he offered no comments. The meeting was soon over and he and Thomas, along with Thomas' father, walked to their homes. As William walked along his driveway, after leaving his friends, he whistled a happy tune. Diana came running out to meet him. They kissed, then walked hand-in-hand to the house. From the porch, they could hear Diana's uncle playing with Marianne. "I thought she would be asleep," he said.

Diana smiled indulgently. "Not until Uncle is too tired to play," she said as they walked through the door. "Marianne, here's Papa!" She called to the child.

William smiled as his daughter laughed, waving her arms at him to be picked up.

Thomas watched Will walk away, amused at his whistling. He smiled at the sight of Diana running out to meet her husband and at she and Will walking together toward their house. He and his father approached Thomas' porch where his mother and Rachel sat in the cool of the evening.

"Come along, Mother!" Called out his father. "It's time to walk home." His mother kissed Rachel on the forehead and took her leave, patting her son on his arm as she passed him. Thomas watched as his parents walked toward their own home, hand-in-hand, just as Will and Diana had been. He stepped onto the porch and sat in a chair near his wife, picking up her hand as he did so.

"How did it go?" She asked quietly.

He looked at her in the silvery moonlight. He could see her swelling abdomen. "They have decided to block the way of the old road to keep people from going up into the fog. It spreads to cover the old village."

She nodded. "It's good."

"It doesn't make you feel sad?"

"Only a little." She paused. "This is my home, now." She rubbed her stomach. "I don't want our children to wander up there into the past. Do you?"

He shook his head in answer. "Our children," he mused. "So, you believe Will, that we will have two at this birth?"

"Yes," she said. "Twins, a boy and a girl."

"He told you that?"

"No," she laughed. "But, I hope so. I hope to have both Ruth <u>and</u> Elijah."

He clapped his hands. "A son and a daughter, all at once! That's quite a dream." He chuckled. "But then, why not? Could anything be more perfect for our new life?"

"No," she answered softly, shaking her head and squeezing his hand at the same time. "It's the perfect ending to my story, don't you think?"

THE END.

Printed in the United States
91682LV00001B/54/A

9 781425 908805